"I'm gonna teach you to throw a lasso, Thena," Jed drawled.

He sidled around behind her, and she felt every inch of her skin pull tight as his hands slid down her arms to her wrists. So this was his tactic, the old touch-and-snuggle method of instruction.

"Now hold it easy," he said as he guided her fingers into position. His breath was warm and fragrant against her neck. "Don't hold too tight, or it might not do what you want. Don't hold too loose, or it'll get away from you."

He ran his fingers up her bare arms as he stepped back. "Go ahead, swing it."

She was so distracted by the tickling warmth that had invaded her body that she let the loop get too big. Suddenly the twirling stopped—the loop had caught Jed around the neck!

"Mercy, ma'am. I'll come along peaceably. Just be gentle when you break me." He stepped close to her and molded both hands to her waist. "Break me, Thena," he whispered in her ear. "Take me apart and put me together again. You've got the power to do it. . . ."

WHAT ARE *LOVESWEPT* ROMANCES?

They are stories of true romance and touching emotion. We believe those two very important ingredients are constants in our highly sensual and very believable stories in the *LOVESWEPT* line. Our goal is to give you, the reader, stories of consistently high quality that may sometimes make you laugh, sometimes make you cry, but are always fresh and creative and contain many delightful surprises within their pages.

Most romance fans read an enormous number of books. Those they truly love, they keep. Others may be traded with friends and soon forgotten. We hope that each *LOVESWEPT* romance will be a treasure—a "keeper." We will always try to publish

LOVE STORIES YOU'LL NEVER FORGET
BY AUTHORS YOU'LL ALWAYS REMEMBER

The Editors

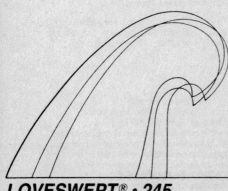

LOVESWEPT® • 245
Deborah Smith
Jed's Sweet Revenge

BANTAM BOOKS
TORONTO • NEW YORK • LONDON • SYDNEY • AUCKLAND

JED'S SWEET REVENGE

A Bantam Book / March 1988

*LOVESWEPT® and the wave device are registered
trademarks of Bantam Books. Registered in U.S. Patent
and Trademark Office and elsewhere.*

ISBN 0-553-21886-7

Published simultaneously in the United States and Canada

---

*Bantam Books are published by Bantam Books, a division
of Bantam Doubleday Dell Publishing Group, Inc. Its trademark, consisting of the words "Bantam Books" and the
portrayal of a rooster, is Registered in U.S. Patent and
Trademark Office and in other countries. Marca Registrada.
Bantam Books, 666 Fifth Avenue, New York, New York 10103.*

PRINTED IN THE UNITED STATES OF AMERICA

O   0 9 8 7 6 5 4 3 2 1

*To Polly, who knows the value of a fine book,
congenial company, and friendly ducks.*

Prologue

"Wait, child, wait! I have to tell you! Trouble gonna fall!"

Startled, Thena Sainte-Colbet lifted her silver eyes and cupped a hand over them to block the intense Georgia sun. At once she spotted a wiry, ancient black woman marching quickly toward her across the scarred wood of the Dundee municipal dock.

Shrimpers and pleasure fishermen eyed the odd, energetic little woman with amusement. A faded print dress billowed about her thin body as she came to a hurried stop at the edge of the creaking planks and looked down, her face scarred deeply with lines of worry.

"You always fret about me too much, Beneba," Thena said in mild reproach. With movements made sure and graceful from years of experience, Thena left her old cabin cruiser's open cockpit and climbed atop the walkabout. She smiled. "I'm going to come over to St. Andrew's and see your new dock tomorrow," Thena added. "I'd visit today, but the pelicans ate five of my tomato plants and I want to set out some new plants this afternoon." She glanced around the municipal docks. "Where did you leave your skiff?"

"Don't turn the subject, child. Don't talk to me like I'm old and crazy," Beneba Everett said in a broken voice.

Thena's eyes flickered with surprise. She quickly

maneuvered her way between crates of groceries and other supplies stacked on the cruiser's creaking foredeck and stepped over the bow railing. Beneba stuck out a scrawny hand and Thena grasped it, frowning as she did. The elderly woman wasn't being playful. She was truly upset.

"Trouble gonna fall!" Beneba repeated. Thena knew that Beneba only slipped into the odd phrasing of the old Gullah coastal dialect when she was very upset.

"Trouble's coming to me?" Thena asked. She shook her head. "Maybe if I lived here on the mainland. But out on the island I'm protected, Grandmother." It didn't matter that their skins were different colors and their families unrelated. Beneba had always been her grandmother.

"I seen it, child. Change in the wind. Trouble is comin'. Not like before, when it found you on the mainland. This time it reaches all the way to your island. I dreamed it."

Descended from Jamaican slaves and Creek Indians, Beneba had a rich heritage of mysticism. She'd been born with a caul over her face. She spoke to ghosts. She also foretold the future, sometimes with disturbing accuracy. Thena felt a chill creep along the back of her neck.

Beneba kept holding her hand, and they sat down together on the hot pine planks. Thena tucked her loose smock between her knees and let her bare legs swing over the green water of the Atlantic.

"What kind of trouble, Grandmother?"

"I don't know for certain. In the dream I heard a man with a voice like low thunder. A man from somewhere far away. He could hurt you and the island. I don't know if he will. I can't tell."

Thena laughed to cover the trickle of fear that ran down her spine. "I'll pepper his behind with buckshot and the dogs will chew his hide. Everyone knows that I can take care of my island and myself. Look,

Grandmother." She pulled a wad of bills out of a pocket in her smock. "I sold four of my watercolor paintings to the tourists today. Two hundred dollars. I'm having good luck, not bad."

Swollen rain clouds pushed in front of the July sun and shadows covered the ocean. Thena squinted toward the horizon, suddenly wishing she were back on the island that lay just out of sight. A gull screamed with a strange note that cooled her tanned skin.

"Child, I'm afraid," Beneba warned. Her pure white hair was wound in a fat braid around her head. When she nodded in rhythm with her words, her braid nearly tumbled loose. "The signs say maybe bad luck, child. Change. The man will come and change everything. You watch out. Keep your eyes to the beaches and the coves and watch for him."

Dark lashes the color of mahogany closed over Thena's narrowed eyes. "No one can hurt me," she said grimly. "When I'm on my island, I'm safe."

The gull screamed again.

"From this man, you will not be safe," Beneba whispered.

"Yep, that's what Sancia is. A haunted island, owned by a witch woman."

"Nope."

Jed Powers looked calmly at grizzled Farlo Briggs, who pressed a surprised, rheumy gaze on him and his answer. Farlo silently steered his fishing boat toward the green jewel of land growing larger on the horizon. Then he spoke loudly to be heard above the chug of the engine and the slap of salt water against the boat's bow.

"Mr. Powers, you sayin' it ain't haunted or it ain't owned by a witch?"

"Both."

"How so? H. Wilkens Gregg of New damn York

used to own Sancia, but we ain't seen or heard from him in forty years. Everybody around here figures it belongs to the witch woman, Thena Sainte-Colbet, now."

"H. Wilkens was my grandpa. He left the island to me when he died last year."

Jed almost smiled at the disbelieving look he got for that bit of information. Farlo's old eyes roamed over Jed's work-scarred hands and weathered face, faded jeans and plaid shirt.

"Son, you sure don't look rich like a Gregg. You don't look like New damn York, neither. And I'll tell you another thing. Them cowboy boots ain't right for island walkin'."

"Reckon that's all true."

Farlo waited for an explanation that never came. The pungent ocean air rushed through the big windows of the boat's canopy, and the engine grumbled beneath their feet. It was a southern July day, but the wind made it temperate.

"You ain't much for yakkin', are you, Mr. Powers? What you're doin' here ain't none of my bizness, is it?"

"Nope."

"You talk funny. Where you from?"

"Wyoming."

"You ever seen the ocean before?"

"Nope."

"Mr. Powers, you sure you want to camp on that damned island for three days? I can come back early."

"Yup. I want to have enough time to look the place over. I don't mean to ever come back again. I'm gonna sell it."

"Well, if you run up on that witch woman, cross yourself and don't look her straight in the eye, 'cause she might put a spell on you. She growed up around old Beneba Everett, and Beneba is a witch. She taught her everything she knows."

Jed leaned in his usual posture—relaxed, but ready

for whatever came his way—against a metal support for the boat's canopy. Standing six feet tall, he had a tough, work-honed frame without a spare ounce of fat on it. Fact and image bespoke a purposeful strength of character and body.

Now he squinted at the approaching island, and his mouth slid into a slight smile. The lawyers had told him when he inherited this godforsaken place that the official caretaker, Lewis Simmons, had died in 1950, and that his relatives had taken up squatter's rights on Sancia ever since.

He'd give this Thena, this last squatter, a few thousand dollars so she could find herself another place to live, and she'd probably be thrilled to leave. Farlo's beer-stained voice broke into his thoughts.

". . . and it's the ghost of Sarah Gregg ridin' that horse on the beach, ridin' just like she did forty years ago 'fore she was killed by a hurricane. Your grandma Sarah was a beautiful woman." Farlo paused for effect as the white dunes and lush forest of Sancia Island began to take specific form in front of them. Jed was surprised to see how large it was. The western beach stretched for at least a couple of miles. "If you see her, you just tell her who you are and she'll leave you be."

Jed arched one brown brow. "I don't believe in ghosts. And if I did, I don't reckon any Gregg family ghosts would want to talk to me." He shook his head. Sancia was Latin for "sanctuary," the lawyers had mentioned. Well, it was sure as hell no sanctuary for him. It was only the relic of an arrogant family that had deserted his mother because she'd married a cowboy with no money. His father. Jed had a score to settle with the past, and Sancia Island was the means to do it.

One

Jed wasn't much of a poet, and he struggled to describe what he felt as he watched the sun sink over the ocean in breathtaking mists of magenta and gold.

It makes me feel good, but sad, he thought. Then he drew his mouth into a grimace of self-rebuke. That didn't make sense. Or maybe it did, and he just felt awkward trying to analyze his emotions. He thought of himself as a simple man with simple reactions, and he didn't like feeling confused, as he did now. Jed had no love for the island, but its beauty made him ache with a wistful mixture of pain and pleasure.

He shook his head at the softheaded thoughts. Bulldozers. That's what this place needed. Bulldozers and construction crews and condominiums for slick, silly rich people.

"Hold on, hoss," he said aloud. "You got fifteen million bucks and an island, so don't go talkin' about rich people. And you're soundin' pretty damned silly yourself at this particular minute."

The spoken words whisked away in the wind, and Jed had an odd sense of having been overheard by something or someone. Feeling uncharacteristically vulnerable, he clamped his mouth shut and listened to waves whisper against the sand a hundred yards away. Huge sand dunes hid his sitting place on both sides, and tall sea oats waved around him like Wyoming range grass. The oats made him feel a little more at home.

Gulls—the noisiest, craziest birds he'd ever seen—swooped and circled against the canopy of the deep, darkening blue sky. A pair of brown pelicans rode the ocean swells like small boats. A breeze caressed Jed's face with the contented sigh of a happy lover.

He shivered for no good reason except that he suddenly pictured his beautiful society-matron grandmother, Sarah Gregg, riding a horse along the white beach that flattened out beyond the dunes. Jed closed his eyes. Damned place is hypnotic, he thought in new dismay. Ghosts, what foolishness that old fisherman talked. . . .

The sound of galloping hooves made him open his eyes.

Jed leapt into a crouching position, his sharp reflexes ready for whatever he might encounter. He didn't know what he'd do if an apparition floated into view beyond the sand dunes, but he'd think of something. Pure craziness, he told himself quickly. There's no such thing as ghosts. But he felt his heart rhythm echo the approaching hoofbeats.

What galloped into view was indeed an apparition, but a living one. Jed heard the explosion of air that swept out of his lungs in relief.

"What the . . ." he began, and stopped. Everything stopped—his breath, his thoughts, his awareness of the rest of the world. In all his thirty-two years, he'd never seen anyone as beautiful.

She rode the dainty little mare bareback, controlling her with nothing but body language and the subtle movements of a rope attached to a nylon halter on the mare's delicate head. A thin white dress, sleeveless and scoop-necked, exposed her slender arms and graceful shoulders. The dress was wrapped haphazardly around a pair of golden, strong legs that clung expertly to the mare's sides.

A trio of tongue-lolling dogs, one small and two very large, circled the prancing horse. An elegant hawk with dark auburn wings nearly the same color as the woman's luxuriant hair hung suspended over her for a moment, then swooped down to the sand and calmly curved its wings against its sides.

A dream. I'm having a dream, Jed thought in awe. He didn't want to wake up.

She slid off the mare and immediately whirled around in an uninhibited show of happiness, her arms spread wide, her head thrown back. The sunset framed her with glowing magic. The dogs barked cheerfully and the mare trotted up and down the beach, shaking her head and snorting. The hawk lazily nudged a periwinkle shell with its beak and fluttered its wings in an attitude of haughty disdain for more boisterous pursuits.

"Thena Sainte-Colbet?" Jed whispered. "Is this my squatter? Great gosh a'mighty."

He tilted his head to one side, his mouth open, his usual squint-eyed toughness replaced by pure enchantment. A second later he felt tickling goose bumps spread from the back of his neck down his entire body. She was undressing.

The white smock fell at her feet and she stood by the ocean completely, beautifully naked, her back to him. With the freedom of someone accustomed to total privacy, she languidly stroked her hands through the dark brown mane of hair that cascaded between her shoulder blades. Jed's body's distinctly male response told him that from this view, at least, she was nearly flawless.

"Thank you, God, for this lovely day!" she yelled toward the blazing sunset. Jed smiled at the sound of her voice—Southern and yet oddly lilting, mixed with some pretty accent he couldn't place. She walked into the waves like a goddess, and when the water swirled around the tapering indentation of her waist, she dove forward and began to swim.

For fifteen minutes he watched in wonder as she cut through the water just beyond the whitecaps. Something might hurt her, he worried. He didn't like swimming, not even in swimming pools, and for sure not in this huge tub of green water. Come out of there, he silently ordered.

When she did, the pleasant but disturbing sensations inside him accelerated. Jed was no stranger to the hot, tight feelings of physical need. But the sight of her wet body, the breasts full and high, water streaming down the gentle slopes and curves into the triangle of dark hair between her legs, brought back his earlier feeling of bittersweet spiritual pain. She rivaled the sunset, making him ache. She was even more beautiful than a mountain wildflower.

His brows flattened in a frown as he watched her limp onto the beach, favoring her right knee in a casual way that told him the limp was an old companion. She worked her knee back and forth for a moment, then walked on, the limp less pronounced.

Even after she slipped back into her dress, he thought she looked beautiful. She slung the water out of her hair with the exuberance of a playful child.

"Let's go home, critters!" she called. Jed shook his head, not believing the quick and loyal way they reacted to her voice. The mare, a unique palomino-roan color with a white mane and tail, waited with absolute stillness as the woman swung up on her back. The hawk rose in the air and led the way back up the beach, and the dogs raced alongside as the mare broke into an easy gallop.

Jed felt as if the light dimmed after the woman and her animals disappeared from view. He sat back weakly and strained his ears to catch every retreating hoofbeat and the slap of the dogs' feet on wet sand. Then he found himself alone again with the ocean and the sunset. Darkness was falling, and he knew he had to get up and walk back to his campsite, a mile up the beach. He had to get up. He had to.

But Jed Powers, born poor and raised hard, a ranchhand and rodeo rider who'd had most of the softness worked out of him at an early age, the son of a hell-raising father who'd taught him never to flinch, began to curse when he realized that he was trembling all over.

"*Ma petites*, there you go. Breakfast."

Thena spread birdseed on the faded gray wood of the windowsill. She stepped back gingerly and watched as tiny wrens gathered there, peeping and pecking for food. She spoke to them for several minutes, this time completely in French.

She loved her father's language. He'd wanted his American wife and daughter to speak it as well as they spoke English, and as a child Thena had enjoyed knowing that on the mainland people used English, but on Sancia she and her parents conversed solely in French. They were special.

Now whenever she used French, she thought of Glynnis and Philippe Sainte-Colbet and felt less alone. Today, worried about Beneba's dream, she needed to have her parents' spirits around her.

Thena tiptoed across old Oriental rugs to her bedside table and deposited her bag of birdseed on the rosewood surface. Work and don't worry, she scolded herself. She had gardening to do, then some painting, and it was nearly eleven A.M.

Suddenly she heard the bounding arrival of canine feet on the front porch. A chorus of barking and whining began, and Thena hurried out of her bedroom. Cyrano, Rasputin, and Godiva stood at the door looking back at her anxiously.

Whenever someone—a misguided group of tourists or hunters thinking to find a refuge from game wardens—slipped onto Sancia Island, the dogs let her know. Today, remembering Beneba's warning, Thena reacted to their alert with a shiver of dread.

"I'll get the shotgun," she told them.

Jed swung his gaze from the trail to the forest around him and back again. With all the savvy of an experienced hunter, he stayed aware of every sound and movement. Squirrels scampered up the pine trees, and he tracked their movements as he walked. Amidst the tall pines and ethereal, twisted oaks, the forest floor was nearly clean here. Where sunlight touched it, he saw a hint of grass growing.

A deer stepped into the sunlight and stopped, watching him without fear. Startled by such unusual behavior, Jed stopped too. They stared at each other for a moment.

Is every living thing here bewitched except me? Jed wondered. He had his wits about him now that sunlight had erased last night's shadows from his imagination. Even so, he couldn't deny a feeling of urgency to find the woman from the beach. She couldn't be as magical as she'd looked. He'd meet her, put that notion to rest quickly, and get on with the business of telling her she had to leave his island.

He walked on, edging deeper into the forest. Sharp-leaved palmetto palms brushed against his jeans, and vines as thick as his muscular forearms twined so low from the trees that he could almost reach up and touch them.

Instinct made him freeze and start to listen a split second before he identified the sound of running hooves and rustling underbrush. Perturbed by the violent speed of the approach, Jed unsnapped the cover on the hip holster that held his small automatic pistol. His hand resting lightly on the gun's rubber grip, he braced his feet wide apart and waited. Ghost or witch or whatever, he was ready.

Thena wrapped her legs tighter to Cendrillon as

the mare leapt through the last barrier of underbrush and slid to a stop in the sandy forest path.
Her heart hammering, Thena gasped with surprise
to find a man standing perfectly still and staring
calmly up at her from just beyond the range of
Cendrillon's snorting nose.

With a quick tug of the rope, Thena backed the
mare a good five feet away from the stranger. He
never moved and barely seemed to blink. She dropped
the rein and slapped the butt of the shotgun snuggly
into the crook of her shoulder, then took aim in the
general region of his kneecaps.

"What do you want?" she demanded. The mare
quieted, only her head moving to indicate her nervousness. Cyrano, Rasputin, and Godiva flung themselves onto the scene and gathered around Cendrillon's feet, growling at the man who never took
his eyes away from Thena's.

"What kind of answer'll make you put that shotgun down?" he asked after what seemed an eternity.
His voice had not the slightest bit of fear in it. It
drawled in a slow way that made her think of warm
molasses and old western movies. She'd never heard
a real person talk this way before.

"Don't play with me," she ordered. Jed lifted one
sturdy brown eyebrow. From any other woman, that
choice of words would have been suggestive. From
her, it sounded innocent and deadly serious, he
thought.

"Well, ma'am, I wouldn't even give that notion a
passin' thought as long as you got that double-barrel
pointed at me."

"You're very wise. What do you want?"

"Well, I came here to talk to a lady named Thena
Sainte-Colbet." He paused, and a trace of humor
glimmered in his eyes. "The witch woman." She
made a huffing sound of offense. "Is that you,
ma'am?" he asked politely.

She hesitated, glaring down at him. "Yes! Go away before I turn you into a newt!"

Jed wasn't certain what a newt was, but for a second he entertained the notion that she just really might be able to make him into one.

"Put that shotgun down before I have to come take it away from you," he commanded in his deep, luscious drawl.

"You talk big for a man alone, on foot, in the middle of my island." The dangerous man would have a voice like low thunder, Beneba had said. Thena shivered. "You're trespassing on Sancia Island. It's private."

"I reckon it's not your island, ma'am."

"You're either very brave or very stupid then."

He was silent for a minute, studying her, thinking— or at least trying to think, looking at her made it difficult—about her accent. "I once met a carnival fortune-teller who talked somethin' like you," he said in a conversational tone. "She was from Louisiana. I bet you're from there too. Which are you, Miss Witch— Cajun or Creole?"

The sudden subject change distracted her, and he inched forward. "Neither. I was born here. My father was French and—stop right there!" Exasperated by his tactic, she pressed the shotgun tighter into her shoulder. "Don't ask me questions. I'll ask you. Tell me what you want! Are you here to hunt? To explore?" Her eyes narrowed angrily. "To steal?"

"I refuse to answer on the grounds that you might blast me with that rabbit knocker."

"I might blast you anyway. You obstinate mainlander, you have five seconds to explain before I sic my dogs on you!"

"I can't talk that fast," he said in that languid voice. Thena thought of Clint Eastwood. The man had hawk eyes and a fascinating face and the same laconic appeal . . . and why was she thinking such nonsense right now?

"Your time is up," she told him.

"Now just hold your britches—" he started. Jed frowned in surprise as the mare suddenly reared. The dark-haired witch woman quickly adjusted her aim, and Jed cursed softly as he realized that he was about to be shot. Shot and mangled, because all three of her damned dogs were coming towards him.

He leapt forward to grab the shotgun away, but too late. It roared with release. The pellets didn't score a direct hit, but several ricocheted off a rock and struck his hand. Jed was dimly aware of the stinging pain as he grabbed Thena Sainte-Colbet, gun and all. The mare jumped in one direction and he pulled in the other, jerking the woman into his arms. They fell down, her scrambling, flailing body on top of his.

"Stop it, you violent rogue!" she yelled, as he shoved the gun away and caught her wrists behind her back. "You awful ruffian!"

He'd never had a woman call him such strange names before, like something out of a corny old movie. Jed almost felt like chuckling until he realized that the mare was going to paw his head off. And judging by the sound of their ferocious growling, the dogs wanted to help her kill him.

"Back!" he instructed the animals in a fierce, authoritative voice. Struggling against his chest, her thighs helplessly straddling his lean hips, Thena thought for a second that even her loyal crew wouldn't trespass on the stony control of the man's voice. He was strong—strong-voiced and strong-bodied—and she might well be at his mercy.

But no. He had to let go of her and cover his head as Cendrillon nearly caught his ear with a sharp forefoot. Rasputin—part Great Dane, part German Shepherd—grabbed one of his hands in a vicious grip. Thena rolled away, gasping for breath. She grabbed her shotgun, sat up, and angled it at his head.

"Back!" she echoed. Cendrillon moved away and Rasputin dropped the intruder's bleeding hand. Jed propped himself on his elbows, his chest heaving with exertion, and stared down the shotgun barrel into her deadly gray eyes. He knew he was trapped.

"Reckon this is where you're gonna leave my carcass for the buzzards," he quipped grimly. "I reckon you've got buzzards on this godforsaken heap of sand, don't you? I sure would hate to be left for those squawkin' gulls and nasty pelicans. But go ahead and shoot me if you have to."

His nonchalant control both impressed and infuriated her. "You idiot," she hissed. "I wasn't shooting at you. I was shooting at a rattlesnake. I should have let it strike you, as it was getting ready to do."

Jed quickly twisted his head as the background noise of the dogs' roaring growls took on new meaning. A few feet away they taunted and snapped at a rattler easily six feet long. After giving up on man for lunch, the giant dog that had bruised his hand so easily was now concentrating on snake for lunch.

Thena looked at the melee too, her brow creased in worry. The rattler slithered into a thick coil and shook its tail viciously. Her heart stopped. "Get back!" she yelled to the dogs.

Rasputin and Godiva—a shaggy, brindled mongrel— moved away from the snake in bounding leaps. But her old beagle, Cyrano, apparently thought it was threatening her. Growling, he darted forward just as the snake struck.

"Oh, no, no!" Thena cried in despair. The rattler clung to Cyrano's throat and the stocky little dog fell down, struggling and whimpering. Thena jumped to her feet and ran forward, ready to shoot the snake. Suddenly the stranger leapt ahead and blocked her way with one outstretched arm.

"Let me by!" she demanded hoarsely.

"Ssssh."

She glimpsed a flash of silver as he retrieved the pistol from his side holster. Thena gasped at the man's speed and accuracy as a crisp, loud pop signaled the end of the rattler's life. It dropped away from Cyrano's throat and the stranger kicked its limp corpse into the underbrush.

Thena numbly propped the shotgun against a tree and sank down beside Cyrano's quivering body. She gathered him into her lap and her stomach twisted in a sick, sinking knot of doom. Trouble had come.

"Old friend, old friend," she whispered brokenly, stroking his head. "My dear little Cyrano. Dear little Cyrano. I think . . . are you . . . oh, there's nothing I can do to help but hold you and love you."

Jed drew long breaths. His bleeding hand hung limply by his side, the pistol still grasped in his large, work-scarred fingers. Watching Thena Sainte-Colbet bow her head and speak to the old dog, he felt self-rebuke and sadness. He was responsible for this.

"Go into the light now, old friend," she said softly. Her heartfelt, simple words touched Jed at the center of his soul and sent shivers through him. He dropped to his heels beside her and fought gruffness in his throat.

"I'm sorry," he said finally. "I . . . God, I'm sorry."

Jed watched her hold her hand against the little dog's side, watched the slow movement of his rib cage stop under her fingertips, watched her fingers float in gentle good-bye over the dog's grayed old head. Her long, dark hair sheltered her face from his scrutiny.

When she looked up at him, he saw only a glimmer of tears. She didn't need tears to convey her sorrow. Her eyes, large and expressive and so very gray that they looked like pearls, tore him apart with a store of old grief that couldn't be expressed in tears.

"Cyrano belonged to my mother," she told him.

"She's gone. Now I feel that another part of her has left me."

"Oh, gal." Her unexpected and intimate confession took him into her confidence for a second and made him feel needed. He'd never realized his rough cowboy voice was capable of sounding so tender. Jed reached forward and pushed her hair away from her face. When he finished, he awkwardly pulled his hand back and reached for the dog's small body. "Let me take him."

"No." Her voice was firm, and a little cold. Jed looked back into her eyes and found the cold reflected there. She had the kind of lovely, intelligent face that told a man his heart would never be safe if she wanted to capture it. Now he saw that his was very safe, as far as she was concerned. "I'll take him myself. I don't need help from a mainlander." She paused. "I knew you were coming. I knew you'd cause trouble. Now go away and take your trouble with you."

"How'd you know I was coming? Who told you?"

"A fellow witch," she said sharply, and gave him a curt, sarcastic look.

Then her delicate lips trembled and she turned her head away, gazing down at the still animal in her lap. Jed grimaced in distress as he heard her hoarse sigh of grief. She rose to her feet, cradling Cyrano's body in her arms, and started down the path.

The horse—what was that funny name it had? Cendrillon? Jed remembered—followed her, along with the two big dogs. He picked up the shotgun and trailed behind with grim determination.

Fifteen minutes later the forest opened, revealing a big, two-story house weathered to oyster gray. Jed glanced over it quickly, surprised at its homey appeal. It sat in the middle of a sandy yard dotted with flower gardens that had been tended by an obviously skilled hand. The tin roof came to a central peak that disappeared under the umbrellalike arms of a giant oak tree.

The house and the porch that skirted all four sides were built high off the ground, on a thick stone base. A set of wide plank steps went up to a porch inhabited by old rocking chairs. He watched Thena carry her dog's body past the house, across the clearing toward the forest on the other side. She turned around and looked at him when he started to follow.

"I'll bury my friend without your help. Go back where you came from." She whipped around and kept walking. Jed halted and nodded to her. But he had no intention of leaving.

When she wearily reentered the yard an hour later, she found him seated on the top of her steps, his arms propped on his knees and his fingers idly toying with a seashell. Thena's quick flare of anger mingled with a disobedient surge of curiosity.

His hair was the color of rich coffee softened with cream, a luxurious brown. It was straight and he wore it moderately short, but it looked untameable, much like the man, Thena decided. His face was as lean as the rest of him, the nose blunt and a little bashed looking, the eyes deep set, the jaw almost too strong.

He was much taller than her own five feet five inches, and old jeans and an equally old short-sleeved shirt encased his taut, athletic body. She looked at his feet and her eyes widened. Cowboy boots? He was traipsing around her island drawling like Clint Eastwood and wearing cowboy boots?

He looked up suddenly, and she retreated behind a wall of reserve. For the first time, Thena noted that despite the rough edges and despite the fact that his presence was unwanted, she had on her porch a very handsome, very unusual man. He stood as she walked across the yard, and Thena hid the discomfort his silent scrutiny provoked. She stopped at the base of the steps and glared at him.

"Why are you still trespassing on my island?" she asked coldly.

For a second his mouth flattened in a line of frustration. Rasputin and Godiva trotted up, growling, and pushed their noses against her leg. The man spoke then, his voice deep and sad.

"If there was any way I could bring your dog back, I would." Thena closed her eyes as his voice produced an unexpected quiver down her spine. "I . . . don't know how to put things into real nice words, ma'am. But I'm just about as sorry as a man can be. I . . . I really am sorry."

She looked up, found him faltering for more apologies and frowning, and wondered what made such a capable and calm man have trouble speaking. Shy? Was this man shy? Thena peered at him closely, and his discomfort seemed to grow. It touched her, and for a moment she could let herself soften towards him.

"It's not all your fault," she said gently. "Cyrano was a . . . stubborn little fellow. He knew the danger." She tilted her head to one side and absorbed the troubled look he gave her. "You seem to be a man who doesn't know how to let his feelings show. Saying that you're sorry is a very great gift for you to give, then. Thank you."

The grateful expression that gentled his rugged face made her glad she'd gone easy on him. "You said the dog belonged to your mother. You got a pa, or is he gone too?"

Thena nodded. "They were both killed in a car accident two years ago."

Jed felt compelled to keep talking, even though he suddenly realized that he hadn't said this much to one person at one time in years. "My folks are both dead too. Mother died when I was five, my pa when I was twenty. But he wasn't around all the time when I was growin' up. I lived with my pa's sister a lot."

"Your pa's sister," Thena repeated. Why in the world was this stranger telling her all this personal information as if he'd been holding it in store for her? He had such an odd way of talking, this mainlander. Nobody along the Georgia coast talked this way. "Is she still alive?"

"No." He shook his head. "Died a few years back." He paused. "See, what I'm tryin' to say is that I know how you feel about your dog. I've had a lot of animals I cared about, but not many folks. My mother and my aunt Lucy were the only people I ever really mourned for."

"That's too bad." When he looked at her quizzically, tears veiled her eyes. "That means you haven't had enough people to love."

Shaken, Jed stared down at her tears and imagined for a second that a woman he'd just met was crying on his behalf. "Reckon not."

Thena *was* crying on his behalf. Abruptly, her shoulders straightened. She didn't understand why this lonesome-looking stranger provoked such a response in her, but she didn't want to feel sorry for him after what he'd done. "Good-bye. I'm going back to the forest." She turned around and stalked toward it. The mare appeared at the edge and waited.

"Are you gonna be all right?" he called. She made a small, impatient gesture with one hand, answering a silent yes. "Don't you want to know why I'm here?"

"No," she called back over her shoulder. "Good-bye. I don't care why you're here. Leave before I get back or I'll shoot you—which is what I should have done before."

Amazed, Jed kept his eyes glued to her as she went to the mare and swung gracefully onto her back. They disappeared into the forest without a backward glance at him. Then he realized he'd never told anyone before that Aunt Lucy and his mother were the only people he'd ever mourned. Jed realized something else—he hadn't even introduced himself first.

She hadn't cared enough to even ask for an introduction. Jed slapped an angry hand against his dusty jeans' leg.

"Damn!"

He'd been bewitched, just as Farlo Briggs had warned.

Two

Thena stayed on the beach until after dark, walking, thinking, grieving. Of course the disturbing mainlander wouldn't go away for good. That was too much to hope for. Her right knee ached a little from the violent encounter earlier in the day, and she sat down to rub the scar that circled her kneecap.

This pain came from a mainlander, too, she thought bitterly—a well-heeled visitor from Atlanta who'd had too much to drink on a warm spring night two years ago. He'd climbed into his Cadillac and gone tearing down the wrong side of U.S. 17, straight into her parents' van.

Thena tried again to remember that night, but as always, her life ended with the recollection of a whimsical haiku verse Nate Gallagher had been reciting to her. Her parents were sitting in the van's front seats, listening. Nate and she were sitting in the backseat, and she had just taken his hand in hers. Then her life stopped.

In the big hospital up the coast at Savannah, a doctor told her that her parents and her boyfriend were dead. The drunk driver went back to Atlanta with a fine and probation. After that, Thena stayed away from the mainland as much as possible.

"The past is gone," she muttered out loud. She was too tired even to grieve now. Thena stood up in the darkness on the beach and wearily called for

Cendrillon. "Cyrano is gone and won't be back," she told herself sternly.

Thena turned and looked toward the forest, toward the quiet glade where she'd scooped out a deep hole in the sand for his resting place. "Good-bye," she said finally, her voice soft and stricken. It was time to go home and await the rest of Beneba's prophecy.

All the next morning Jed debated the words to use when he talked to Thena Sainte-Colbet again. There was no solution but to walk back through the forest to her house and confront her as diplomatically as he could. Trouble was, he didn't know diplomatic words; he knew plain, straight words.

He spent the whole morning procrastinating and planning while he explored the island's beaches, picking up seashells. Even mundane clamshells fascinated him, because he'd never seen a shell except those glued to plastic ashtrays in tourist shops. He took off his shirt and boots, rolled up the faded legs of his jeans, then stretched out in the shade of a gnarled pine tree on the edge of the sand dunes to examine his finds.

At midafternoon he ate a meal of crackers and Spam, put on his shirt and boots again, and walked into the forest. Today no welcoming party met him, and he went straight to the rambling old house.

"Ma'am?" he called through the screen door. No answer. Jed cupped his hands around his eyes and squinted into the dark, cool interior. He saw heavy, upholstered furniture that had endured a lot of years. Packed bookcases lined almost every wall. Jed noticed that the big room included a huge dining table and a kitchen in one corner. Large, open windows, their shutters pulled back for the summer, let in filtered sunlight and the constant island breeze.

It was a friendly place with pine plank walls painted white and cheerful print curtains. A high ceiling and a central hall combined to draw air through the house and keep it cool. Jed felt the delicious breeze against his back as he stood at the front door.

"Thena, you home?" he called again, louder. Speaking her name out loud for the first time gave him a pleasant thrill. Jed idly tested the screen door, and it opened. This was, after all, his house. Everything on Sancia Island was his except for the personal effects left by Lewis Simmons, the caretaker his grandfather Gregg had hired forty years ago.

Jed stepped into the cool house, feeling a little guilty nonetheless. He was a deeply private man, and he respected other people's privacy, but he also itched to look at everything that had to do with Thena Sainte-Colbet.

He walked slowly around the main room, scanning the bookcases. Now he remembered that Lewis Simmons had been some sort of scientist who studied plants. And the lawyers had mentioned something about Simmons's daughter and her husband doing the same kind of work. These books showed that.

Jed stopped by something so odd it made him whistle under his breath. A big color television console occupied a corner of the room like a visitor from another planet. Jed ran his blunt-tipped fingers over the VCR unit that sat on top of it.

He'd walked around the house yesterday to look at the cistern for catching rainwater. Next to it he'd found the shed that contained the gas-run generator that provided electricity. Thena lived in isolation on a deserted island, but she had a color TV and a VCR. It made no sense, but then not much else here did either.

Shaking his head, Jed crossed to a half-shut door and pushed it open. His lips parted in an involuntary sigh of admiration.

Her bed was cradled in a heavy, antique frame made of some sort of reddish wood. Miles of white net draped over it from a central fastening on the tall ceiling. Fancy rugs covered the wood floor under the bed. It was a fantasy scene that made sensual images of her leap into his thoughts.

"Great gosh a'mighty, I've never seen anything like this in my life," Jed murmured. Absolutely enchanted, he sat down in a rocking chair across from the bed and waited.

Thena came in the front door five minutes later, a sketch pad in one hand and a bucket of shells in the other, with her sandals positioned on top. Softly singing a song from an old Judy Garland film she'd rented a week ago, she put her things on the thick oak dining table and padded toward the bedroom.

Her voice, nearly in tune, rose heartily as she stepped inside the room and inhaled the scent of hibiscus outside the open windows. Thena began to pull her smock over her head. Then she made a half-turn to her right and saw yesterday's stranger seated in her mother's rocking chair. Rocking.

Jed caught one glimpse of her golden, naked rump before she snapped the smock down and backed away, her eyes full of molten silver, her lips parted in shock.

"We've got to talk, ma'am," he said as politely as he could, considering that he didn't know which he felt more—embarrassment or arousal. Didn't she ever wear panties or a bra? "Whether you want to or not."

Her beautiful face became a mask of fury. "Get out of my house," she said evenly. "You voyeuristic interloper."

Jed stood up, determined to be pleasant but straightforward.

"I apologize for interlopin' around here," he said wryly, "but the fact is, ma'am, this isn't your house."

"You, cowboy, have been out in the sun too long. Go!" Thena pointed toward the bedroom door and wished she hadn't left the dogs outside and the shotgun on the porch.

"Would you just read somethin'?" Jed reached in a back pocket and brought forward a legal document. "This ought to explain everything—"

"Out!" she ordered, stabbing the air with one hand in the direction of the door.

Jed was getting more frustrated by the moment. "No." He held out the document. "Read this, dammit, and calm your feisty self down."

Thena glared at him in utter rage. This was her sanctuary, her home, her island, and she'd had enough of this rough man, handsome or not. She started toward the door. He blocked her way so quickly and gracefully that she yipped in startled dismay.

"No gun and no dogs," he ordered, reading her mind. Jed held out the document in supplication. Thena's gaze darted toward a bedroom window that opened onto the front porch. She caught the subtle movement of the man's body as he balanced to block that exit, too. Real fear began to gnaw at her.

Jed saw it and winced. "Now, look, don't be scared of me. All I want is for you to read this paper and talk to me about it." And I'd like to know if you sleep naked and alone in that big old bed over there, he added silently.

Thena relaxed a little at the earnest sound of his voice. She eyed the document for a moment, then jerked it out of his hand and popped it open. Jed shoved his hands into his back pockets and watched her intently as she read.

Jed felt a wistful little pain curl around his rib cage as her defiant expression faded and the pink undertones drained out of her honeyed complexion.

"Oh," she whispered weakly. "Oh, I see." The look she turned up to him was blank with disbelief. Then she frowned and tilted her head to one side to study him. "My mother was raised here. I was born here." She pointed to the bed. "Right there. That's all that's important."

"Folks are born in hospitals, but that don't mean they own 'em." She looked at him with slowly rising anger, and he put his hands on his hips. He hadn't meant to sound so flippant, but dadgummit, she had to listen to reason. "Nobody from the Gregg family ever told you this was your island, did they?"

"No, but after all these years . . . My parents were scientists, and they said H. Wilkens Gregg meant for Sancia to be preserved, and that one day he'd get around to donating the island to the state as a wildlife refuge. We always knew that would happen."

Jed shook his head slowly, without any attitude of victory. " 'Fraid not, ma'am."

She frowned. "Just who are you?" She read the document again. "Jedidiah Huntington Powers? Is that you? You're Mr. Gregg's grandson, cowboy? You?"

He nodded. "Don't have to make it sound so hard to believe, ma'am. And it's Jed Powers. Nothin' fancy." "Huntington" came from Huntington Wilkens Gregg, and he hated that.

"All right, Jed Powers. Why are you here?" She closed the document slowly and handed it back to him. Abruptly, she smiled. "Are you going to donate the island to the state?"

Jed nearly groaned. "No."

Her smile faded. "What are you going to do with it, then?" Trouble gonna fall, trouble gonna fall, Beneba had said.

There was no way to soften the blow, Jed thought wearily. "Sell it for development." She gasped. "But don't you worry. Now listen—"

"No!" She snatched her hands to her throat in an expression of horror, and his heart sank all the way to his boots. She shoved out of the room past him before he could stop her. "Rasputin! Godiva!"

"Hold on, now!" he yelled, and leapt after her. Jed managed to throw himself in front of the screen door before she could reach it. She slid to a stop, her eyes narrowed with fierceness. Jed thrust his chin forward. "Don't you dare sic those dogs on me."

"I'll let them teach you a lesson in morals, you indiscriminate greedy oaf." Her voice came out low and trembling with anger. "You'll go back to the mainland with their fang marks in your behind."

"Are you trying to make me do something mean?" he asked.

Thena backed away, her hands still touching her throat in distress. "Such as?"

"Something. You'll be sorry, if I have to." Jed studied her fear and instantly added, "I don't want to, Thena."

"Don't call me by my name. I may not own Sancia, but I own my name." Her shoulders sagged. The light died in her eyes and Jed felt terrible for her. "Just go," she said dully. "I have to think."

"You can't hide from the facts, Thena . . . ma'am. We might as well talk about the future."

"You're horrible." Her voice made that simple description sound like a lethal curse. "Get out."

"Nope. I don't want you to think I'm some sort of mean hellion."

"This island is part of my family heritage! And . . . and your family heritage!" she said fervently. "I know all about the Greggs—my grandfather told me. H. Wilkens and Sarah honeymooned here. Their daughter was born here. Their daughter . . ." Thena stared at him. "Your mother?"

He nodded grimly.

"The old Gregg mansion is still here." Thena held out pleading hands. "If you could just see it . . . if you could just see SalHaven—"

"Hell, no. I don't give a tinker's damn about the Gregg family and I want to be rid of this fancy playpen of theirs."

New words died in Thena's throat. Jed Powers's voice hadn't risen and nothing overt had changed about him. But his dark eyes now froze the world with disgust and anger.

"You," she said quietly, "are an angry man with a cold heart." Thena straightened with rigid dignity and indicated the door behind him. "Get out. I won't turn the dogs on you. Just leave."

Jed couldn't remember when frustration had threatened his calm nature so badly. Frustration and wounded feelings, all because this woman called his heart cold. She made him feel cruel, and he wasn't.

"This is my house," he said slowly. "And I'll stay if I want to." He paused, his chin jutting forward. "You got that . . . Thena?"

She exploded into action. In two quick steps she reached her dining table and grabbed a ripe peach from a stoneware bowl there. Jed didn't even have time to duck. She hurled the peach with a force that amazed him. It bounced off his ribs with a painful thud and left a soggy stain on his plaid shirt.

"Get out," she repeated, and reached for another peach. With typical calm Jed looked down at his aching side, then back up at her.

"That's real good," he said dryly. "But since I never heard of a man bein' killed by a peach, I'm sure not a helluva lot scared."

"You will be." The second peach flew across the room and smacked him in the jaw. Jed grunted with surprise and pain, but held his ground. He gingerly touched his jaw and couldn't argue with the possibility that peaches might be fatal.

"Now there's no need for gettin' rowdy," he murmured soothingly. "Let's talk." Thena paused, off guard. He charged her.

"Cheat!" she screamed.

Thena grabbed two more peaches and ran to the far side of the large table. Jed flung himself across it, scattering shells and knocking the bowl containing the rest of the fruit to the floor.

Thena screamed again as his hands grabbed for her skirt. Pelting him in the head with another peach, she leapt away. Her hand shook badly around the remaining peach it held. Heaven alone knew what this forceful man would do if he ever caught her. Trouble, trouble.

"Stay away from me!" she cried.

"I've had all I'm gonna take from you. I want an apology."

She uttered something in French that Jed figured was distinctly not an apology. Deadly silent, his face white with pain and anger, he rolled off the far side of the table and charged toward her again. The bottom of his left boot made contact with a slick chunk of peach on the wood floor, and his left leg decided to take a different direction from the rest of him.

Thena gasped as he tumbled energetically backward and whacked the side of his head on the rim of the kitchen's yellow Formica countertop. His eyes closed in obvious response to the sharp torture, but he made no sound. He simply slid to the floor in a sitting position, his back against the kitchen cabinets, one denimed knee drawn up. He slowly flattened a hand over the rising lump on his head, and the skin around his mouth lost some of its ruddy color.

"I want to die with my boots on," he mumbled, his eyes still squinted shut. "Just go ahead and beat me to death. Get an ear of corn. That ought to do the trick."

"Dear God," Thena said slowly. How could he joke when he'd nearly brained himself? Somewhere deep inside her, grudging admiration flared along with the fear that he might be seriously hurt. She dropped her last peach and hurried to the kitchen sink, where she soaked a dishcloth in cool water.

"Sit still," she ordered. Thena knelt beside him and tentatively reached out with the cloth. His eyes opened, their gaze directly on her. He spoke somberly.

"I'd rather be beat to death than smothered, ma'am."

He had a way about him that was funny and outrageous, and she was too overcharged to react in a reasonable way. Thena couldn't contain a little smile at his humor.

"You're safe for the moment."

She quit smiling and pressed the cloth to the top of his head. He lowered his hand as Thena squeezed the soggy material. She watched the brown of his hair darken to chocolate as the water soaked it.

"Maybe that will help. Are you bleeding?"

Jed continued to study her as he ran his fingers under his wet hair. He pulled them away and she glanced over. He had absolutely battered hands, covered in scars and calluses, and the little finger on this particular hand was a tiny bit crooked, as if it'd been broken and hadn't healed right. His hands suited what she knew of his nature, she decided. They intrigued her.

"No blood," he answered.

"Good."

"You're bein' mighty concerned about my health all of a sudden."

Thena gave him a warning look. "Don't bet on it. I just don't want your carcass to foul my island."

She began to wipe peach juice off his face, her ministrations a little rough and impatient. Hazel eyes, she thought suddenly. He has beautiful, deepset hazel eyes. And he smelled sweaty and masculine in an erotic way that drew attention from some traitorously female part of her brain.

"How old are you?" he asked abruptly. She nearly dropped her cloth. Thena cocked one dark brow at him.

"Twenty-five. Why?"

"Just askin'."

She began wiping his face again, but now she felt very uncomfortable. His weathered complexion was red from the rough cloth; her fingertips accidently brushed his skin and the texture of his fine beard stubble transmitted strange signals up her arm.

"How old are you?" she asked just as abruptly.

"Thirty-two. Why?"

She pursed her lips in exasperation. "Just asking. You look older than that. It's all those cowboy squint lines." Thena tossed the cloth onto the countertop above him. "There." She sighed with deep fatigue. "I'm afraid you'll live."

"You hate me," he said evenly. "And I reckon I don't blame you."

They shared a long look and both of them blushed. The word "hate" provoked a confusing intensity, Thena thought. Her mouth tightened into a straight line. "Give me any reason why I shouldn't hate you. I'm going to fight this plan of yours. I'm going to go to the state conservation people and ask them to get some sort of legal order against you."

"Fair enough. Fight, then. But when you talk to those folks, do me one favor, huh? Don't say I'm sellin' the island just to make money. I'm not, 'cause I've got more money now than I know what to do with. So don't make me out to be a hog. I'm sellin' this place because I don't intend for it to be some sort of do-goodin' monument to my old hypocrite grandpa. He was spiteful and mean."

"You're spiteful too, cowboy. That's a sad way to live your life."

"You want me to feel different, you give me good reason."

"All right," she answered tautly. "I'll give you a tour of the island that will knock your boots off."

Jed nodded, accepting her challenge. "I have to leave late tomorrow afternoon, but between now and then you show me around and I might keep an open mind." It wasn't a lie, he assured himself. He might. "Whatever I decide, I want you to know I sure hate that you're takin' this so personal."

She fended off that disturbing comment with an impatient wave of one hand. "So tell me where hard-headed cowboys such as you are born and raised."

"Wyoming."

Thena looked at him as if he'd said "the moon."
"Ah, now I see. You couldn't possibly understand
what this island or any other island is all about."

Jed nodded. "Never saw an ocean or an island,
before yesterday. Don't care to see one again. You
ever been West?"

"I visited New Orleans once, when I was a little
girl."

Jed looked at her from under his brows, the look
conveying deep worry.

"That's not West," he noted dryly. He mimicked
her. "You couldn't possibly understand what I'm all
about."

"New Orleans is west of here. It qualifies."

He chuckled. Thena tilted her head and absorbed
the gentle, warm sound. It invaded her body and
loosened all her muscles with disturbing ease. Certain parts of her body enjoyed the experience even
more than others.

Jed abruptly stopped chuckling when she leapt
up, frowning at him.

"Get on your feet and go back to your campsite,"
she demanded. "I have painting to do. I'll see you at
dawn."

"I'm camped—"

"I know where you're camped. Cendrillon and I
watched you all morning from the forest."

Startled, he retorted, "See anything interestin'?"

Thena nearly blushed again. She'd seen him strip
his shirt off, and the sight of his hairy, muscular
chest had been very interesting.

"No. How can you stand to wear those hot jeans?"

Jed stood up slowly. Now he towered over her, his
body only inches away from hers. "I can take the
heat," he said in a provocative way.

Thena stepped back from him, her heart pumping
too hard, her facial muscles rigid with her determination not to show the confusion she felt. Why was

he staring at her lips? Was he actually contemplating a kiss?

"I have a lot of questions to ask you," she told him.

"I'll try to answer 'em, if you'll answer mine."

"Tomorrow." Thena replied. She was suddenly frantic to get him out of her house. He was using what Nate had somberly called "primitive sexual innuendo," and she was shocked. For years she'd tried to provoke such a display from Nate, until she'd finally admitted that she just wasn't sexy enough.

She hadn't attempted to provoke Jed Powers at all, yet he was standing here singeing her with a look that was about as primitive as an innuendo could get. Her breath seemed to have trouble finding its way into her lungs. Very slowly, he leaned towards her.

"Tomorrow," he echoed. He tipped a finger to his forehead in a gesture of good-bye that was old-fashioned and oddly gallant, then turned on his bootheel and strode out, swinging the screen door shut behind him with a jaunty slap of his hand.

Thena sank weakly into a chair. She wasn't going to let Jed Powers sell her island. She'd capture him one way or another—if he didn't capture her first.

Three

Uhmmmm. When had he ever felt this languid? When had waking up been so slow and so full of pleasant dreams? Jed smiled, then rolled over in the sleeping bag so that the cushion of sand was under his back. He took a deep breath and inhaled a sensual feast of sea air mixed with food cooking over a driftwood fire.

Cooking? Fire? Instincts honed by years of light sleeping—mostly listening for his father to stagger drunkenly up to the door of their tiny trailer—brought Jed instantly awake. He stared up at the canvas canopy that protected his eyes from the sunlight, then jerked his head to one side and found the source of his dreams. Thena.

She sat cross-legged a few feet away, tending a skillet over his rekindled campfire. The morning light tinted her pink, and the constant ocean breeze lifted strands of her untamed hair. The ripe swell of her breasts was just visible under her white T-shirt, and short white shorts emphasized the golden tautness of her legs.

Jed felt an ache of physical desire, and greedily took the secret moment to memorize her face feature by feature. She had a delicate nose that could have belonged to a fancy debutante with cool blue blood and white-gloved hands, Jed thought. Her cheekbones were just as haughty, high and well-defined. She reminded him of all the rodeo queens who'd sought him out when their daddys weren't looking.

But her mouth and eyes, Lord, they took away any hint of snobbery and turned her into an earth mother, a pirate's woman, warm as hot cider and twice as sweet. Her nature was quicksilver expressions and animated movements, and she made him feel even quieter than he was. But it felt good to be her opposite; it felt right.

Jed became aware of the texture of his lips, wind-hardened and tight from too few smiles, and he wondered how her gentle, full mouth would feel against them. She made him think of roses, of their softness and sweet smell. Thena began to sing some silly old movie song very softly, and Jed succumbed to pure reverence. He watched the tiny movements of her dark lashes, now half-lowered to protect her eyes from the brightening dawn light. The woman had magic in those eyes, and he needed magic in his empty life. He lay there without moving, transfixed by the simple beauty of her silhouetted against the dusky pink sky and white sand.

Then she saw him watching her. Her song stopped and her lips remained parted, curved in an oval of embarrassment.

"Good morning," she said finally. "I hope you like fried whiting and wheat biscuits."

Thena's strained nerves produced a flood of odd and vaguely pleasant reactions in her body as he lay perfectly still without answering and kept his disconcerting gaze trained on her. Do cowboys dislike fish? she wondered. Or is he angry about yesterday?

She forced herself to remain immobile under the quiet, dreamy gaze he gave her. She'd never watched a man wake up before, and now she wondered if other men besides Jed Powers had such dark, sexy eyes in the morning. How could a man with a rumpled face and disheveled hair be so attractive?

"Thena, is this breakfast a bribe?" His voice was rumpled too. It teased her with mellow good humor and dispelled her fears.

"Yes." Smiling, she nodded vigorously and looked back at the pan of floured whiting filets sizzling in oil. "I went through your food supply. Crackers and Spam are no diet for a day of island exploring."

"Might nosy, aren't you, gal?"

Gal. What a strange, likable word, she thought. "Your backpack was open. And I still consider this my island. I'll do what I want."

They traded challenging looks. Abruptly, still teasing, he smiled at her. Abruptly, she smiled back. Fingers of golden light poured over the treetops, and Jed shivered with emotion as the whole world seemed to light with Thena's smile and the morning sun.

"Great gosh a'mighty," he said softly.

"What's wrong?" She cocked her head to one side and looked bewildered.

Jed fumbled to hide his emotions. "It's . . . is it always so durned bright here in the mornin'?"

She laughed, to his delight. "Isn't it bright in Wyoming?"

"Not like this. Here it's like everything's sharper and clearer than I've ever seen it before."

"That's not just from the sunlight." She smiled mysteriously. "That's from inside you." She reached over and pointed to his heart, then quickly brought her hand back to her lap. "Sancia has a way of making your heart open up to everything around you."

Jed chuckled. Now she was talking nonsense. "Why, I thought I was just havin' a spell of indigestion."

She held a spatula in her other hand, and after a moment she shook it at him. "You'll see," she warned tartly.

Thena turned back to her cooking and tried to ignore the rapt attention his eyes still lavished on her. "Last night I looked up articles about Wyoming in my *National Geographic*s. No wonder you feel out of place here. What part of Wyoming are you from?"

"Little town called Hard Chance Creek. Up in the mountains."

Thena nodded, recalling photographs of craggy peaks and swirling blizzards. "You'll just have to give yourself time to adjust." She offered a kind smile, as if he were a heathen she would convert for his own good.

"So you think I just need to be brainwashed?"

"No. You need your consciousness raised."

"It rises by itself, thank you, ma'am." Chuckling, Jed unzipped his sleeping bag and slid from under the canopy so he could sit up. Thena was aware of her pulse hesitating as she got a close-up view of a prime male body covered by nothing but snug jeans. Why, he's beautiful, she thought.

His chest had a thick covering of curly hair, and the hair remained thick as it flowed across a stomach terraced with small muscles. Nothing was soft about him but that dark brown hair, and she imagined how silky it would feel to her fingers if she touched it.

Which, of course, she had no intention of doing. Not just because of the conflict between them, but because she didn't ever again intend to touch a man in a sexual way. Any man. With that thought came embarrassing memories of Nate's rejections.

Jed felt her scrutiny as if her fingertips were tracing every inch of him. He grabbed a T-shirt from the backpack near his feet and hurriedly slipped it over his head. She could burn a man up with those eyes, he thought. How many men had she turned to ashes before him?

"I'll take your breakfast bribe," he said gruffly. "It puts cowboy food to shame."

"Good. Here's another bribe." She reached for something hidden on the other side of her and handed him a pair of scuffed leather sandals. "Wear these today and leave those hot boots behind."

"These look like somethin' an old hippy would own."

"They belonged to my father, and he most certainly wasn't an old hippy," she retorted. "He was a member of the French Olympic equestrian team when he was young. And he was a well-respected marine biologist. My mother was a biologist too, by the way. So you'd better wear those sandals with pride."

He made himself look very chastised. "Yes, ma'am." His firm mouth crooked up at one corner. "I just thought maybe they belonged to your last boyfriend."

She looked at him for a moment, and the shaming memories of Nate rose in her mind again. Oh, yes, she had no doubt that she'd best ignore her sexual feelings. Nate had said many times that she was an intellectual being not suited for intimacy. Her fumbling, unsuccessful attempts to change their platonic relationship over the years had done nothing but make him more certain they both should remain celibate, and finally she'd had to agree. She was a thinker, not a lover.

"Now that . . . friend," she said slowly, "was an old hippy. But he wore tennis shoes, not sandals."

Jed trained his eyes on his feet as he slid them into the strange-looking shoes, which were a little too big. He kept his voice and his expression poker-playing neutral. "What happened? Did you blast your old hippy boyfriend with the shotgun for some reason and chase him off?"

"He wasn't just an old hippy. Before he came to the coast to live, he was a university literature professor. He was also a philosopher. Very brilliant. He died in the car wreck, with my parents."

Jed raised apologetic eyes. She gazed back at him without rebuke, but after a minute he murmured, "Sometimes I can put both of my big feet into my big mouth. Forgive me?"

Thena nodded, and her eyes filled with puzzlement. He sounded so kind and sad. It was getting difficult not to be fascinated with him, even if he were here to cause her nothing but trouble.

Jed absorbed the flicker of affection in her expression and felt as if she'd kissed him. Goose bumps ran down his arms.

"Were you in that accident too?"

She nodded and pointed to her knee. His eyes roamed over the network of surgery scars, and he remembered her limp. "It happened on the mainland," she explained calmly. "That's one reason I love my island. No cars except an old truck I use to haul supplies. No drunk drivers." She paused, and her gaze turned bitter. "Your island," she corrected.

Guilt surged through him. "I wanted to tell you yesterday, but you never gave me a chance, gal. You can keep your house and the land around it. Looks like you don't have enough money to move anywhere else."

"Thank you," she said coldly. "But I do have money. My parents left me a little and I paint watercolor seascapes that bring in enough for most expenses. Money's not the issue."

Jed frowned, his generous gesture shot down. She put several golden whiting filets on a china plate she'd brought with her and unwrapped a dozen biscuits bundled in aluminum foil at the edge of the fire. She put three biscuits on the plate and handed it to him. Jed accepted the hot dish without looking at it.

"You can't expect me to keep this place," he protested. "What does a cowboy need with an island?"

"You'll change your mind." She nodded with an attitude of profound wisdom. There were beautiful spirits here—Sarah Gregg's chief among them—and good powers of love and serenity that would capture his heart no matter how much he resisted. "This place is special." She pointed to his plate. "Eat, and I'll try to explain why."

Jed nodded. His thoughts completely distracted

from food, he took a bite of the wheat biscuit and noted dimly that it was buttery and hot and wonderful. His woman was beautiful and very smart—he could tell that by the educated insults she had flung at him in the past two days—and a fantastic cook. Oh, yes, and she read *National Geographic*.

His woman? Great gosh a'mighty. He mentally kicked himself back to the real world, where scruffy cowboys, even rich ones, didn't win the affections of island princesses.

"Sancia Island," she began, "is nearly thirty square miles in size." Thena wrapped her arms around her updrawn knees and looked out over the ocean. "It has ten miles of virgin beaches. Loggerhead turtles come here to lay their eggs. The forest is full of wildlife." She leaned forward and touched his arm, her eyes gleaming with almost maternal pride. "I have indigo snakes here." When he didn't register recognition—he couldn't think about much else other than the pressure of her warm fingers on his skin—she looked dismayed. "Those aren't found anywhere in the world except on these barrier islands, Jed."

Jed. He liked his name for the first time in his life, because she made it sound lyrical.

"All that'd still be here," he told her blankly. "We'd work it out." Something had softened his vengeful desire for bulldozers and condominiums, he realized in the back of his mind. Jed knew as soon as he got away from here and her that he'd set his revenge on course again.

She released his arm and shook her head a second time. "No development. None at all. That's what you're going to have to concede." Thena thought for a moment, then looked at him with renewed enthusiasm. "Horses! That's what you need to see! Did you know that your grandmother kept Arabians here?"

"No, I never cared to learn what she did. I'm a quarter horse man, myself. Arabians are a might too dainty for my tastes," Jed muttered. Her enthusiasm wilted. "But pretty," he quickly added.

"Magnificent." she corrected. "Your grandfather left them after Sarah was killed. When he went back to New York, he took his little girl—your mother—with him and left the horses and everything else. My grandfather told me all about it. And we always wondered what became of the little girl."

"She fell in love with a dirt-poor cowboy named Roarke Powers. She married him and they had a son. A few years later she died an ugly death." Jed held up a warning hand to stop the flow of shock and curiosity into Thena's eyes. "Tell me more about the horses."

Shaken, Thena assessed the old resentment and deep pain that simmered underneath his hard exterior, and she felt sorry for him. This man hadn't had an easy life.

"The Arabians," she continued softly, "bred with our island horses. The island horses are the descendants of horses left here by the Spanish, back in the sixteen hundreds. They bred with the Arabians over the past fifty years, and the combination produced some wonderful foals. The herd numbers about twenty-five head. My parents sold horses to the mainlanders, occasionally."

"Tell me about Cendrillon. I've never seen a horse that reddish palomino color in my life."

Her eyes gleaming, Thena smiled. "She's the best. I watched her being born and that makes her even more special to me. My father taught me how to train horses, and I put everything I learned into training her."

"What's that name of hers mean?"

"It's old French for 'Cinderella.' She was stunted and ugly when she was born, and no one except me ever thought she'd grow out of it. She had hidden beauty."

Thena continued talking about Cendrillon and the island's other animals for several more minutes. When she finished, Jed seemed mesmerized, as if he couldn't think of anything to say. Finally he told her in a low voice, "You love everything here, I figure, and everything here loves you. I see why."

Thena caught her breath. How could the man put so much sexiness into such ordinary words? This conversation could quickly get out of hand. She stood up and jabbed a finger at his half-eaten food. "Yes, well. Hurry and eat. I'll call one of the other horses up for you. I've trained a few besides Cendrillon."

"You just want to watch me get stomped by a half-wild stallion," he joked. "But I made my livin' for a lot of years ridin' rodeo broncs, so don't get your hopes up."

"Why did you stop competing?"

"I got stomped by a half-wild stallion." He smiled a little and pointed to his neck. "Cracked two verte-brae. That was when I decided to train quarter horses for a livin'. Right now I'm huntin' for a ranch to buy. I'm gonna have the best quarter horse ranch in the country, one of these days."

"That costs money. You must have inherited a lot." She looked at him in a disapproving way that told him exactly what she thought of his sour atti-tude toward a family that had done him the favor of making him rich.

That was a mistake. His eyes immediately hard-ened. "It was my mother's money, meant for her." Jed squinted up, and his deep voice cut her attitude to shreds. "If she'd had it years ago, she'd still be alive. I didn't ask for the money or this island, but I got it. And I don't feel one damned bit bad about havin' what should have been hers."

Thena felt her face turning pink. "I . . . there's probably a lot I don't know about all that," she said hurriedly. "And it's none of my business. I didn't mean to sound judgmental. All I care about is what you intend to do with my . . . the island."

Jed's anger dissolved under her earnest response. "I reckon I look real bad to you, and I'm sorry about that. I don't expect you to understand the way I feel about this old Gregg family place."

Thena measured the stoic quality in his voice and the strong resolve in his face, but behind his hazel eyes she believed she saw genuine sadness on her account.

"You don't look bad to me," she told him. Why she wanted to soothe this man's feelings, she didn't know. Thena sighed in dismay at her jumbled emotions. "You just look like a mainlander who has to be educated."

"So teach me, gal."

For a breathless second they stared at each other in awkward anticipation—anticipation of what, Thena didn't want to consider. She began backing away.

"Eat," she urged. "I'll go get the horses."

Jed watched her until she disappeared into the forest. You don't look bad to me, she'd said. He felt like a half-grown boy on the verge of giving a giddy whoop.

Thena knew the minute Jed settled onto JackJaw's buckskin back that she was in the presence of a man who understood and loved horses as well as she did. Already astride Cendrillon, she watched Jed expertly guide the stallion in loping circles on the beach. JackJaw wore nothing but a blue nylon halter and rope reins.

It was a powerful sight, lithe man and fluid horse moving so gracefully together on her beach, and Thena felt sweet tears rise under her dark eyelashes. Jed Powers couldn't be heartless enough to sell her island—it was impossible. His expression was serene and his smile was honest. Honest and very attractive.

She became aware of molten warmth shimmering through her body. She suddenly seemed too hot, as if she had her own internal sun, and when a bird trilled in the pines nearby, she felt an odd, poignant emotion race up her spine. She thought her island had strong powers. Well, perhaps this unusual man had powers too. His last name might be appropriate.

Jed slid the stallion to a halt beside Cendrillon, and Thena smiled weakly at him.

"You understand horses," she said.

"Been ridin' since I was in diapers."

"You must have used a lot of baby powder."

"Itched like a sonuvagun."

He grinned at her and the sun inside her nearly went nova. Deep lines etched his eyes, his strong jaw softened, his whole handsome self became an example of Mother Nature's intention that men should be irresistibly attractive for the sake of the species. Thena stared at him with unabashed rediscovery.

The horses stood so close that her bare knee met the taut rope of muscles in Jed's thigh. JackJaw shifted, took a step forward, and her knee slid sensuously along the surface of Jed's outer leg. Thena was shocked to find out that her knee contained an erogenous zone.

Apparently his leg was even more affected than her knee, because his grin faded and she sat, hypnotized, as he studied her intently.

"You make a fine horse trainer," he said gruffly. "This stud moves like he's been taught to step between eggs without breakin' them." Through a subtle movement of his leg, he eased JackJaw a few inches away from Cendrillon. Thena shivered with relief.

"Let's go," she said abruptly. "I have a lot to show you."

"I'm ready and waitin' to be shown."

She gave him a long, assessing look, then nudged Cendrillon toward the dark mysteries of the forest.

Jed half-expected elves to pop into sight at any minute, then huffed at his foolishness. He began to feel the way he had as a boy, sitting next to Aunt Lucy in church. He felt like whispering.

They were in an area of huge, twisted live oaks covered in lichens and Spanish moss and ferns. Clumps of palmetto bushes rattled against the horses' legs; magnolia trees hung paddle-leafed branches out to caress Jed's arms and face. Thena rode beside him, and from time to time she made comments about the island.

"What's that nice smell?" he asked.

"Bayberries and wild grapes. I always think of Tasoneela and Gabel Boisfeuillet when I smell it."

"Who?" Jed inquired, as she had hoped he would. Now she'd catch his imagination for sure.

"Tasoneela and Gabel Boisfeuillet. They were lovers here back before the Revolutionary War. They died on the island."

"From eatin' bayberries and wild grapes?"

Thena clucked her tongue in dismay. "Don't make fun. Do you want to hear the story? If you believe in spirits, you'll like it."

"I believe in spirits like Jack Daniel's and Johnnie Walker." Jed smiled ruefully at the piqued look she gave him. "But I like ghost stories."

Thena nodded and tried to be patient. He thought he knew so much. Mainlanders always thought they knew so much.

She inhaled slowly and began. "Tasoneela was a beautiful Indian girl." Thena pulled her shoulders back. "She was strong and courageous and proud." She glanced at Jed and found his eyes directly on her. Best to look away from those eyes of his, she thought quickly, and did. "The Spanish held this coast then, and they took anything they wanted from the land and the Indians. One man, a cruel captain named Miguel de Leturiondo, wanted Tasoneela." Thena arched one brow in feminine disdain. "To be his mistress."

Jed would have smiled at her melodramatic style, but he was too charmed by it.

"He came to her village to take her, but Tasoneela escaped." Thena held out both hands to the island. "She traveled to Sancia to hide, all alone. A year passed, and she fell in love with her island. Even alone, she was happy." Thena lowered her voice. "Then one day she found a badly injured man, nearly dead, lying on the eastern beach. He was a French pirate named Gabel Boisfeuillet, and his ship and crew had been destroyed by Spanish forces."

She cleared her throat. Despite every intention he had of remaining cynical, Jed felt his pulse hesitate every time she paused for effect.

"Keep goin'," he ordered.

"Tasoneela was afraid of him, but she couldn't bring herself to let him die. She cared for him, and when Gabel regained consciousness and looked up into her sweet face, he fell in love. Tasoneela learned quickly that her handsome pirate was a man worth loving in return. Gabel begged her to leave her island and travel the oceans with him, and for love's sake, she did."

Thena paused again to take a deep breath of fragrant air. "And?" Jed asked immediately. "What happened?"

Thena repressed a victorious smiled. "Tasoneela loved Gabel, but she missed her island. She was desperately miserable, and Gabel couldn't bear to let her suffer. He brought her back here and stayed with her. They were going to farm the land."

Thena stopped talking as she gently shooed a butterfly away from her face. "What happened?" Jed demanded.

"Miguel de Leturiondo learned that Tasoneela and a French pirate were living on Sancia, and he sent a detachment of soldiers to capture them." Thena pointed to the north. "They trapped Tasoneela and Gabel on the beach near that end of Sancia. Gabel stood in front of her, protecting her with his body, and fired at the soldiers. Several fired back, and a bullet killed Tasoneela."

She paused again. Jed leaned towards Thena without realizing he was doing it. "Was Gabel killed too?"

Her face somber, she nodded. "He asked the soldiers to kill him. They refused. But they let him carry Tasoneela's body to a glade she'd loved, and he buried her there. He asked them again to kill him, and this time—touched by his grief, and knowing that torture and hanging waited for him on the mainland—they did. They buried him next to Tasoneela."

Thena looked quietly at Jed and was pleased to find belief in his expression. Then he began to come back to reality a little, and his dark eyes gauged her with mild suspicion.

"Is that tale true?" he asked, almost smiling.

"It is. I swear." Thena was sincere. She'd heard the story of Tasoneela and Gabel so many times and from so many people that she had no doubt it was true.

They rode in silence for several minutes, Jed assessing the strange feeling of wonder her story evoked, Thena assessing Jed. The forest floor began to slope downward. Abruptly the horses stepped into a cove surrounded by the dense woodland. Deep, shimmering water beckoned with soft arms of sand. A murmuring creek wound back through the forest from it.

Jed breathed in the cool, sweet air of a heaven on earth. The elves, he was sure, would appear at any minute to greet Thena, their goddess of the woods.

She slipped down from Cendrillon's back and walked to the water's edge, her senses acutely aware of every sound as Jed jumped down from JackJaw and followed. She sat in the warm sand and he sat also, very close beside her. Too close. That primitive sexual innuendo again, she thought with a quiver.

"This is it," she whispered. "This is where Tasoneela and Gabel are buried."

His heart pounding, Jed twisted his head and

looked at her in surprise. She met his gaze and his pleasant, musky breath touched her face. Her lips parted slightly as she inhaled his life, his nearness.

"Here?" he murmured.

Thena's nerve endings felt stretched by the magnetic pull of his gaze, and suddenly she knew she'd made a terrible mistake by telling him the lovers' story. Not only had the story captured him, it had captured her as well. Her pulse raced, and the insides of her thighs, already made sensitive by Cendrillon's coarse hair, tingled.

"Here," Thena said breathlessly. "Sometimes . . . sometimes I hear them laughing . . . I think they made love here." She couldn't stop looking into the seductive depths of his eyes. "I'm going to call you Jedidiah from now on," Thena whispered.

A look of bewilderment and delight came into his face at the abrupt announcement. "I'm too ordinary to be a Jedidiah. Jed suits my plain nature better. But thank you."

Thena shook her head very slowly, never taking her eyes from his. "No, Jedidiah. You see yourself through harsh eyes. I don't."

"Oh, gal, you're sweet talkin' me for this island's sake."

"No." Her eyes shamed him with their rebuke. "I don't play flattery games. I don't know how."

Jed lifted his chin proudly. "I don't know how either."

"Then believe me. I see the beauty in you, Jedidiah."

Jed did the only thing a man in love-at-first-sight could do, given such encouragement in such a romantic setting. Lost in her serious eyes, lost in the flowerlike scent of her body and her gentle insistence that he was beautiful, he leaned forward and settled a kiss on her startled mouth.

Four

The warm, firm feel of his lips pressing tightly to hers was a foreign sensation that stunned her. Thena kept her mouth clamped shut, and she knew—or at least she thought—that she wasn't kissing him back. But she felt herself succumbing. Perhaps she was Tasoneela, reborn under another identity to fall in love with a reborn Gable Boisfeuillet who came to her in the guise of this weathered horseman.

She came to her senses and started to move away. Jed's hand rose to her cheek and his callused fingers touched her skin almost reverently. Despite his aura of implacable calm, his fingers trembled. A puzzling sense of pleasure filled Thena as she realized that he was trying to calm her, that he was telling her that he meant her no harm. She wanted to trust this Wyoming pirate. She wanted to keep kissing him.

Rational thought left her as the skillful movement of his mouth sent shivers down her spine. A mixture of surprise and confusion made her heart race wildly. Thena had no idea a man's kiss could be this overwhelming. None of the prim lip contact that passed for kissing in the old movies she rented had prepared her for the hot, liquid feeling that threatened to burn her from the inside out. She pursed her lips against Jed's tentatively, and he encouraged her response by moving his mouth over hers in a capricious series of caresses.

Her mind blank, her eyes squinted shut, she ducked her head to escape the intriguing smell and taste of him. For a second her mouth was free, and she gasped for breath. Her voice came out crisp and rebuking. "The aggressive male tendency to dominate is a sign of—"

"Pure friendliness," he drawled softly. "I'm not tryin' to dominate you, I'm tryin' to kiss you."

Thena's head jerked up at the teasing sound of his voice. She met his hazel eyes and found them darkened by sexual urgency. This cowboy knew how to look at a woman with disarmingly honest need, she thought dimly. He was just a lusty, basic example of mating capabilities—and she was going to sit very still and let him kiss her again.

Which he did, and this time his tongue slipped forward and nudged the center of her lips provocatively. What did he want? she puzzled. Thena's hands, clenched in her lap, jumped with alarm as she understood. French kissing. She'd read about it in the sex manuals she'd bought when she was trying to unravel the secrets of Nate's resistance.

Oh, no, she didn't know how to kiss like that, and she wasn't going to make it obvious. Part of her simply didn't intend for this laconic Lothario to be amused at her clumsiness, and part of her ached with humiliation, knowing that she didn't have the skill to give him the pleasure he sought.

Thena scooted away from him, her chest heaving with sudden anger. His fingers trailed away from her face and hung in the air for a moment, as if reaching for her. He frowned mildly, looking concerned by her sudden change of heart.

"I didn't bring you here to . . . to spoon with you," she said firmly.

"Spoon with me?" His mouth widened in a flat smile at the archaic term. "Spoon?"

Thena's face flushed with embarrassment. It was a word she'd heard Jimmy Stewart use in *The Glenn*

Miller Story a few nights earlier on TV. Cloistered here on her island, she didn't know the current slang for what Jed had just done. Now she knew it wasn't spoon. "Whatever you want to call it, I didn't intend to make you think I'm interested in a physical relationship with you," she retorted.

What Jed lacked in verbal skills, he more than made up for in solid instinct and observation. He could read a horse's mood just by looking into its eyes. It was the same with women, and he knew that this island wildflower, for all her protests, had enjoyed his touch, his kiss. He didn't know if he could tease her into caring about him, a cowboy with too many rough edges, but the kiss made a good start in the right direction.

"Do you have a man?" he asked bluntly.

Her eyes narrowed in defense. "No. Should I?"

"Well, most gals put a high value on us handsome devils."

"I find value in things other people don't understand," she informed him. "I paint pictures of sea life with a detail most artists don't care about. I'm also an amateur scientist. I spend a lot of my time making intricate notes about the island flora and fauna. I send them to a biologist at the University of Georgia."

Thena sighed dramatically. "I just don't have time to indulge in superficial sexual encounters. Sexual attraction is nothing more than a complex interaction of hormonal chemicals, anyway. It's been tested many times in laboratory experiments."

Jed grunted. "When I kissed you, wildflower, your lips weren't thinkin' about white mice."

"My chemicals were simply reacting to yours." She and Nate had discussed this subject in great detail. Jedidiah Powers couldn't confuse her.

"Uh-huh. Like a volcano. You were scared to kiss me back the way you wanted to." His eyes held enormous self-satisfaction. "Guess you thought your chemicals might boil over."

Thena decided to take the offensive. "Do you have a woman?"

"Not lately."

"Well, I refuse to fill the temporary gap in your lurid sex life." She was surprised to see a wounded, soulful look pass briefly across his face. Thena kicked herself mentally. This man didn't fit her idea of a lecherous playboy, despite his bold attentions. He looked as if he'd spent most of his life on the outside looking in at everyone else's happiness. She was a loner too. She understood.

Thena's anger faded. "Jedidiah," she murmured, her musical voice putting beautiful inflections in his name, "you're a very handsome man. And I have no man in my life." He looked askance at her frankness, then his eyes filled with intense respect for it. Respect, and affection. Thena's lips parted in a melting reaction to such rapt attention. For a moment she simply stared at him, feeling a little giddy. Finally she forced her eyes away from his and continued. "But I'm just . . . just too old for romance, you see."

He nearly choked on a restrained laugh. "You look mighty fine, granny."

"In here," she said plaintively, as she pointed to her head.

"Whew, that's a relief," he teased. "I thought maybe you'd put a spell on me so I couldn't tell that you're about a hundred and toothless, with pruney lips." His amusement died as he saw all the pain behind her silver eyes. "Why are you too old?" he asked gently.

Thena forced herself to ignore the effect his rumbling, tender voice had on her emotions. "I never had a chance to make many friends my own age. I went to elementary and high school on the mainland, but I didn't really fit in. I was too quiet, and I liked to read all the time, or paint. I was very close to my parents, and I spent a lot of time on Sancia with them and various colleagues of theirs who'd drop by here to do research. I went away to college for a year, but I decided I could learn more on my own than in class so I came home. Now I know that was a mistake."

She pointed to her head again. "So . . . I'm old. I like to watch movies, I like to read, I like to be alone. I've never been on an airplane, I've never been to a rock concert, and I've never watched MTV."

"You haven't missed much on any of those three counts," Jed observed wryly. He paused. "But even a sweet little old lady like yourself needs those chemical reactions you were talkin' about. What about your friend? I bet the professor didn't think you were over the hill."

"Nate Gallagher," she offered. Jed had unknowingly picked just the subject to cement her argument. "He said I was an ancient intellect. That's even more intense than 'old.' "

Jed considered her strange comment for a moment. Surely this Nate hombre hadn't treated such a vibrant lady like an aging book. If he had, he was a fool. "Well, Miss Witch, you may be ancient between the ears, but you're well-preserved on all other counts." He reached a hand out to touch her, but she shook her head and moved farther away.

"I can't, Jedidiah. I won't. It's nothing personal, so don't be offended. I find you very attractive, which is a great compliment considering how much trouble you've caused me."

"Would it be different if we weren't at odds over this island?"

"Are you hinting that you'd trade Sancia's future for my physical affections?"

He stood up quickly, and Thena followed. The fire in his eyes would have soldered metal. "No."

"I'm sorry, Jedidiah. That was an ugly thing to assume. I don't know much about this sort of thing . . . how men go about it, I mean."

"Go about what?"

"Courtship." Thena watched the amazement register in his lean face. "Uhmmm, not courtship, I know that means something serious. Flirtation. Yes, that's it. I'm sorry I misinterpreted your routine sexual flirtation for something manipulative."

Her straightforward manner was as mesmerizing as it was exasperating. Jed ran a hand through his brown hair. "Wildflower, there was nothin' routine about it. I never met a gal like you before, and I don't expect to ever meet a gal like you again." He hesitated, annoyance growing inside him. "I don't like playin' word games with you. And quit treatin' me like I'm a damned bug you're studyin'." His tone was full of warning. "If you're so scared of courtship that you have to call it something else, then that's your problem." He turned and stalked toward the horses.

Thena gazed after him in weak surprise. No, no, she thought desperately. He can't court me. I don't know how to be courted. I don't even know how to kiss.

They rode on through the forest in silence, both of them somber. Jed tried to distract himself by picturing bulldozers ripping into the green glades, scattering the palmetto plants and the flowers, plowing down the huge oaks and their canopies of moss. The only problem was, if he let that happen, this beautiful woman would hate him until the day she died. He winced at the idea.

The thought of invoking hatred had never disturbed him before. As a kid on the rodeo circuit, he'd been tough in defense of himself and his father. Roarke was blustery, outspoken, and often drunk, a bad combination that usually got him into more trouble than he could handle alone.

So from the time he was big enough to fight, Jed had come to his father's aid. Over the years, more than two dozen men had cursed Jed's name viciously. He knew that on rainy days those men rubbed at the twinges of arthritic pain in their jaws and cursed his name anew.

A few of his father's ne'er-do-well girlfriends probably still hated him too. As a kid, he'd locked them out of the trailer he and Roarke shared, put snakes in their purses, hidden their clothes—anything to drive them away from his father, whose soft heart for the female gender often made him a patsy for unscrupulous women who needed money or a place to stay.

Jed rarely turned his bitterness toward his father. He had a deep sense of compassion, though few people cared enough to notice it, and he understood that a lot of Roarke's behavior came from a sense of having lost everything when Jed's mother died. Amanda Gregg Powers had tamed him for a few years, but after her death he spiraled toward oblivion with single-minded disregard for the consequences. He had died in a drunken knife fight in Tucson, Arizona.

A commotion on the right of the forest trail brought Jed's attention back to the present. Out of a big rhododendron flew a gawky, bottom-heavy bird with a wingspan easily five feet across. It lumbered upward and disappeared over the treetops.

"A wild turkey," Thena explained. Jed looked at her and found her smiling toward the piece of sky where they'd last seen the monstrosity. "Wasn't he beautiful?"

"Sure. Just like a flyin' elephant. But if you say he's beautiful, then I'll agree."

"Why, thank you," she said primly. "Courtship has made you a more likable human being."

"You're welcome. Now about this courtship—"

"You're going to see a wonderful sight, Jedidiah." She intended to keep this conversation on impersonal ground. "Close your eyes."

"Oh, no." He slapped JackJaw's neck ruefully. "This little stud is probably trained to throw me when you give some hand signal. I don't trust you."

She laughed. "Close your eyes. I'll lead JackJaw." She reached over and took the nylon line from Jed's hand. He arched a brow at her and attempted to assess the situation.

"This is silly. I don't like to play games," he grumbled. A blush began to creep under the tan on his neck.

"That's too bad, Jedidiah. You need to learn to relax." Actually, he looked as if he was never anything but relaxed, Thena thought in dismay. He reminded her of a lazy, watchful wolf, always conserving his energy for the hunt. "Please. I want you to enjoy the full effect of what you're about to see."

"Oh, hell, all right." Feeling very uncomfortable and unprotected, he shut his eyes and put a hand on each taut hip, trying to maintain a nonchalant attitude.

"Oh, you're so trusting." She chuckled. "What a sucker."

"You got thirty seconds, gal. And it better be good."

"It will be." She led JackJaw beside Cendrillon, guiding both horses out of the forest onto the edge of what had once been a magnificent rolling lawn. "Smell the air, Jedidiah. It's sweeter here because there are dozens of magnolia trees."

He inhaled the scent, and it brought a disturbing, poignant feeling into his chest. There was no world beyond this world, no voice other than Thena's, nothing more important than staying here, near her. For the first time in his life, he felt at home. The sudden and unexpected idea threw him for a loop.

"Just a few feet farther, Jedidiah. Keep your eyes closed."

"We're outside the woods now, aren't we? We're in some kind of clearin'."

"That's right. Listen to the grass rustling around

the horses' knees. Doesn't it sound like whispers? The island spirits are whispering about us."

"They're sayin', 'Look at that idiot with his eyes shut.' "

She laughed in delight. "No, they're happy that you're here."

"No, they're not." He was serious.

Thena stopped the horses side by side. For a second she fingered Cendrillon's white mane nervously, hoping that what Jed was about to see would make all the difference in his feelings for Sancia. She reached over and touched his forearm. The hard muscles tightened in response.

"Now, Jedidiah," she said softly, "keep your mind and your heart open. Promise me you won't say anything for a while. Promise me you'll just be quiet and absorb what you see. It's only fair."

"My mind's open, my mouth's shut, I'm absorbin'. Okay, I promise."

"Then look at your mother's home."

Shock ran through him as his eyes opened. Every muscle inside him twisted with emotion. Part of it was anger, but part was curiosity too. "Damn," he said under his breath.

SalHaven stood in the distance with all the wistful dignity of an aging Southern belle. She was closely surrounded on both sides by suitors of live oak who nodded to her deferentially as the breeze moved their gnarled limbs.

Thena listed architectural details in a calm voice, ignoring the knot in her stomach. "SalHaven has three stories. Before the 1945 hurricane destroyed the left end of the house, there were twenty rooms— ten guest bedrooms, a master suite with a bedroom and a living room, servants' quarters, two kitchens, a formal living room, a formal dining room, and a ballroom. The style is a mixture of classical Greek and Federal. You might say it's like Tara in *Gone With the Wind*—but instead of big columns across the front, there's a one-story portico above raised staircases. You can still see two of the chimneys. There were three. The third was on the side that the hurricane destroyed."

Thena gestured gracefully with one hand. "These overgrown lawns and magnolias—see the old flower beds everywhere—my grandfather said this used to be beautiful. Your grandmother Gregg's Arabians used to graze out here. On the back side of the mansion, there's a semicircular pavilion of white marble. You can almost see the ocean from it. The rest of the house is built of gray blocks made of cement, sand, and crushed seashells from Sancia's beaches. Think of it, Jedidiah. It's as if SalHaven rose from the island. It's a part of the island. It's not imposing at all, for such a big place. It has a very warm aura. The outbuildings and your grandmother's big stable are gone. The hurricane got them—"

"Too bad it didn't wash the whole damned place away," Jed interjected curtly.

Thena stared at the hard set of his face and the dark distaste in his eyes. Her head drooped with disappointment. "You promised to be quiet and keep an open mind."

"I didn't expect for you to bring me to this fancy hellhole without a warning. That's not fair. I didn't want to see it."

"You promised," she said hoarsely. "This is where your mother spent her childhood. Don't you at least want to go inside, for her sake?"

He turned brooding eyes on her, studying the way her expressive features molded themselves in sadness. She already held a power over him that no one else ever had, and he couldn't bear to leave that wistful pain on her face. "For your sake," he muttered. "I'll go inside for your sake."

A little stunned, Thena simply nodded.

Her grandfather, the caretaker hired by H. Wilkens Gregg, had boarded up the mansion's windows and doors forty years earlier, but the wood had fallen away from the main entrance. They left the horses to graze on the front lawn. Curving stone staircases flanked the portico on both sides, and Thena led the way up the left set. She glanced at Jed out of the corner of her eye, watching him as they stepped through the tall, arched entrance into a spacious foyer. He looked tense and unhappy.

"Italian tile," she said wearily, and pointed to the dirty floor. "It's a beautiful oyster color underneath all this grime. When I was little, I used to come here to play. I scrubbed these tiles with a brush once, just to see how pretty they were."

"You weren't scared here?" Dappled sunshine came through cracks in the boarded windows and the open door, making odd patterns on the peeling walls. Jed listened to the slight echo of his voice in the empty rooms.

"No. I've never felt afraid of SalHaven. It has a serene atmosphere that I enjoy."

"Good spirits, huh?" He sounded sarcastic.

"Yes." Her chin up, Thena walked down a hallway and stopped outside a triple doorway easily ten feet tall. Jed's breath caught at the ethereal sight she presented, standing in the shadows. She belongs here, he thought suddenly. This old house loves her.

He rebuked himself for such nonsensical thinking and followed her. They entered a big, empty ball-room, and Jed couldn't help but feel awed. Plaster crumbled from the high walls and the ceiling, and the patterned marble floor was cracked in places, but the room had a grandeur that reminded him of the Greek ruins pictured in school books.

"Grandfather said this room used to have a beautiful crystal chandelier almost twenty feet in diameter," Thena commented. "It was sold along with all the other furnishings, after your grandmother was killed in the hurricane." She pointed to the far side of the ballroom, which was open to the elements.

"There used to be five sets of French doors with beveled glass across that side of the room. They were sold too. The opening was boarded over, but the salt air and wind finally destroyed the wood, just as it did the wood that covered the front doorway."

"What's that outside?"

"The pavilion. It's magnificent. I've read newspaper accounts of the parties your grandparents used to give here, and the writers always mentioned that guests loved to dance outside."

Jed walked onto the magnificent curving porch. Its ornate marble columns were interspersed with filigreed marble benches. Overhead, in a vaulted roof, the remnants of stained-glass skylights framed jagged squares of blue sky. At the left end of the porch, where the hurricane had wreaked its damage, the roof had crumbled. Only a large pile of rubble and broken columns remained.

"Look past the edge of the pavilion," Thena instructed. "See where the formal garden used to be? And if you squint across the marshes farther out, you can see the beach dunes. That crumbling foundation over to your right marks where the stable was. It had forty stalls, Jedidiah. Can you imagine? And beside it, stretching for three hundred acres back into the forest, were the pastures. The oaks have taken them over now, but"—Thena swung around in a circle, her arms out—"can't you see SalHaven the way it must have been when your mother was a little girl? I can see her playing here, right here on this pavilion. She must have had a fantastic childhood."

She swung around again, smiling, and met Jed's gaze. Then she saw the sheer grief and fury in its hazel depths. He looked as if he wanted to tear SalHaven apart with his bare hands.

"Don't hate her father so much," Thena begged. "Don't take that foolish hatred out on SalHaven. Don't ruin Sancia because of some misdirected bitterness—"

"You don't know anything but fairy tales and sec-
ondhand stories." His voice was terribly strained.

"Tell me the truth, then. I don't know what happened to your mother. Tell me."

His struggle to find the right words was painfully
obvious. A muscle quivered in his jaw. He put his
hands on his hips and stared tensely out at the
overgrown gardens.

"You don't have to be eloquent, Jedidiah. Say what
you feel."

"Her family killed her."

"How?" Thena asked in a stunned voice.

"She met my old man at a charity rodeo and ran
off with him. She was a fancy socialite and he was
livin' hand-to-mouth on the rodeo circuit. But by
God, they loved each other, even though nobody
understood why. The Greggs had a fit, especially her
father. Pa told me old H. Wilkens actually hired men
to come get her, but they were too late. By the time
they caught up with her and Pa, the two of them
had been married a month.

"So they beat the hell out of Pa and went back to
tell H. Wilkens about the marriage. H. Wilkens never
forgave her, even though she begged him to. When I
was five years old she took me to New York, tryin' to
get in to see the old bastard. I guess she thought
he'd soften up when he saw his grandson."

Jed walked slowly to the edge of the pavilion, turned
his back so that his emotions were hidden from
Thena, and leaned against a column. The rigid control in his posture brought tears to her eyes.

"What happened?" she asked gently.

"He wouldn't even see her. I was too little to remember much of what happened, but I'll never forget sittin' beside Ma on a bus headed west. I'd never
seen her cry before, but on that trip home she cried
for hours. That was when I started to hate my
grandfather."

"But what did it have to do with—"

"She got pregnant again, and she had problems from the beginnin'—mostly, I figure, because Pa was laid up with a hurt back and she was workin' two jobs to support us. She called H. Wilkens's sisters and asked each of them for a loan, but the old biddies told her they wouldn't meddle in their brother's feud by takin' sides with her. Ma had too much pride to ask her father for any money, so she did without. I don't think Pa ever realized how much she did without."

"How did she die?"

"She got something like blood poisoning."

"Toxemia?"

"Yeah. That's what they called it. She fainted in the kitchen one night. Pa put her in the truck and I held her head on the way to a hospital, but that place transferred her to the public hospital because she was a charity case. She went into a coma and died in a roomful of other patients, without even a damned privacy curtain around her bed."

"Oh, Jedidiah." Crying silently, Thena hugged her arms across her chest. He was no longer a stranger. He was a deeply hurt man whom she understood very well.

His voice was rough. "And old H. Wilkens had the gall to raise hell after she died. He tried to have her buried with the rest of the Greggs, in New York, and Pa had to go to court to fight it. Then he tried to get custody of me, for God's sake. I guess he wanted to hurt us as much as he could." He paused, and all the energy seemed to desert him. His shoulders slumped. "That's the kind of man who built SalHaven."

"A man who loved his daughter and his grandson and tried to show it in the only ways he knew how."

Jed turned around slowly, every movement lethal with tension. He looked at her with disbelief. "I don't want to hear that kind of . . . I don't want to hear it."

Thena held out both hands. He had to consider

the possibility that his grandfather was a decent man. "Don't you see?" she asked. "He probably would have helped your mother if she'd come to him for money. After she died, think of the guilt and regret he must have felt for what he'd done to her! He wanted to make everything up somehow. Bringing her body home and raising her son in luxury must have been his only hopes."

"You're just tryin' to save this place by talkin' nonsense."

Wounded, Thena brushed the tears off her cheeks and straightened angrily. "The fact that your grandfather left you Sancia Island and millions of dollars ought to prove how desperate he was to make amends."

"Maybe he got religion right before he died. Lost of hellions do."

"No! I don't feel that kind of presence here at SalHaven," she argued. "I've heard stories about your grandparents all my life. Your grandfather had too much pride, but he wasn't a monster. He just didn't know how to accept a daughter who had an equal amount of pride. It's sad, Jedidiah. You should feel sorry for him. . . ."

Jed uttered several choice swear words in a low, furious voice. Thena froze, staring at him wide-eyed, afraid of the raw anger she'd provoked. He closed in on her like a predator, his movements so quick that she had no chance to run. His hands shot forward and grabbed her by the shoulders, then twisted her around to face the cool, empty majesty of the mansion's interior.

"Let me go!" she ordered tautly. He pulled her against his chest so that he could put his mouth close to her ear. Thena struggled against the heat of his breath, the harsh power in his body, the carefully controlled strength in his hands. He spoke fiercely.

"Look at this place and tell me I should feel sorry

for that bastard," he demanded. "This was a palace. He was a king. He could do anything he wanted. It wouldn't have hurt him to forgive my mother. To hell with feelin' sorry for him. Don't you ever say that to me again."

Philippe Sainte-Colbet had noted on many occasions that his only child had the temperament of a wild mare. Thena jerked away from Jed Powers's possessive hands and turned to glare up at him with pure menace, her breath coming in short swallows. "You have no right to touch me," she warned.

"I have a right to everything on this island," he retorted.

She twisted on one sandaled heel and walked quickly inside the mansion. Jed followed her, silently cursing every confusing, upsetting thing that had occurred in his life during the last three days because of her.

She went outside with him close behind, signaled Cendrillon, and swung up on the delicate little horse's back. She scowled down at him and spoke in a cold voice. "What would you like to see next, cowboy? Or does it matter? You never seriously intended to let me change your mind about selling my island, did you?"

"No."

He watched her fingers wind tightly through strands of Cendrillon's long mane. "You were just playing with me, making fun of me," she accused. Her gray eyes were molten with fury. "Maybe you thought you'd make friends with me and then I'd be no trouble at all. You'd get a . . . a little pleasure and then you'd leave. Was that it?"

"Sure," he said tautly. "I was just going to use my country-boy charm to sweep you off your feet. Savage and Slick, those are my middle names."

"Good-bye and good riddance, cowboy." She backed the mare away from him and swung her around in one smooth movement. Thena looked back over her shoulder at Jed. His expression was inscrutable, but she thought she saw sorrow in his eyes. She forced the notion away. "I hope you can find your own way back to the dock on the west beach," she told him in an unconcerned tone of voice.

"I reckon I can manage that simple chore without your help. You're not goin' to sic your devil dogs on me, are you?" Rasputin and Godiva had just trotted out of the forest, and they eyed him greedily as they panted by Cendrillon's legs.

"No. I'll find other ways to fight you."

"Fight me, and you'll lose everything."

Thena gave him a look full of bitter irony. "Your grandfather would be proud of your attitude."

She swung the mare around and nudged her into a lope. The dogs followed. Jed's shrewd gaze stayed on her until she disappeared into the sanctuary of the island woods. That sharp-tongued gal is right, he finally admitted in disgust. He sounded just like the grandfather he hated.

By the time she reached her house, Thena had settled on a dangerous plan. Everything had gone wrong at SalHaven, and the island's future looked grim because of it. She had to take desperate measures, even though they might provoke the brawling side of Jedidiah's nature.

Thena went into her bedroom and sat down at a ham radio on the small table near her bed. Jedidiah had mentioned that he'd hired Farlo Briggs to bring him over to the island and take him back. She got a telephone connection via her radio and punched Briggs's number into her phone base.

When he answered, she said politely, "This is Thena Sainte-Colbet on Sancia Island, calling for Jedi-di . . . Jed Powers. Mr. Powers has decided to stay on the island a few more days. I'll call you when he's ready to return to the mainland."

There was a very indecisive pause on Farlo's side of the connection. "You ain't bewitched him, have you?" he asked suspiciously.

"Not yet," Thena deadpanned. "He was perfectly normal the last time I saw him. He simply changed his mind about leaving today."

"Uh-huh," Farlo mumbled. "Well, call me when he's ready to come back."

"I certainly will," she said cheerfully. "Good-bye."

After the connection clicked off, she opened the radio and looked inside. "Frequency synthesizer board, where are you?" Thena muttered under her breath. Her nimble fingers located the tiny board and removed it. Being serendipitous had its advantages, she thought. Not many people understood the inner workings of a ham radio better than she did.

Thena went to the vanity dresser in one corner, found a safety pin, ran it under a component lead, and secured the board inside the waistband of her baggy white shorts. Even if Jedidiah knew how to operate a ham radio, even if he broke into her house and forced her to show him the radio, it'd be a cold day in Dixie before he got the radio to work without the little darling that lay cool and flat on the skin beneath her navel.

Smiling, Thena sat down in her rocking chair and simply waited for all hell to break loose.

Five

Dusk was gathering around the short Sabal palms in Thena's front yard before Jed's pride crumbled and he pounded on her screen door. Rasputin and Godiva trotted to the door and sat down in front of it, facing him grimly. Jed returned their threatening gazes.

"Yes?" Thena called lightly, as she walked up the hallway from her studio at the back of the house. With all the nonchalance of a housewife answering a salesman's visit, she wiped her watercolor brush on a white rag and gave Jed an inquisitive, innocent examination.

He propped one hand on the outside doorframe and leaned jauntily, the other hand on his denimed hip, Clint Eastwood in distress. His expression was grim. "I'll give you fifty dollars if you have a radio on this godforsaken lump of sand and you'll use it to call the guy who was supposed to come get me."

"Why don't you stay on Sancia a few more days, Jedidiah? I'll give you a room and plenty to eat. I'm sorry I took you to SalHaven before you were ready."

His deep voice was tense, but she heard the apology in it. "Seein' that old place brought back a lot of memories. You just got in the middle and caught the flack. I wouldn't ever have been so mean . . . I think a lot of you and . . ." He broke off, unable to express what he was really feeling. Thena's heart softened a little.

"I understand. You . . . you just fired from the hip."

"But that doesn't change a thing about the way I feel toward the island. All right, you can keep your house and the land around it, but I'm gonna sell the rest to a developer."

Her voice never rose. "You might be tougher than whale skin, but I'm a match for you. You're not thinking clearly. The rhythm of life here will mesmerize you, if you just give it a chance."

"A hundred bucks. Just call Farlo Briggs and I'll give you a hunded bucks."

She took a steadying breath. "I've already called him. He'll be back for you in a few days. I'm afraid I've taken you prisoner."

Her heart thumped painfully as he straightened, his face tightening into a mask of disbelief and anger. Those dark hawk eyes assessed her through a squint that focused his anger into a searing ray. "Nobody," he emphasized, "has—ever—taken—me—prisoner."

"Until now."

"Thena." His voice was dangerously slow. It vibrated with tension. "Call—Farlo—Briggs—before—I—get—mad."

"Maybe my radio is broken. Maybe my boat won't start. It's perfectly logical."

He slammed the screen door open and lunged toward her, but the dogs met him with bared teeth and raised hackles. He stopped, his legs braced, his hands clenched by his sides. Thena's hands were shaking as she held them out in supplication.

"You might as well accept your fate. It won't be bad. You can sleep in my old bedroom upstairs. We'll go back to SalHaven tomorrow and—"

"Call Farlo," Jed interjected, biting off both words with clenched teeth.

She shook her head. His expression turned darker, and he took one more step forward. Rasputin darted toward him, growling, and snapped viciously at his leg. Godiva posed to leap. "Stop, Jedidiah, please!" Thena begged. "They'll attack, and I won't be able to stop them before they hurt you!" Jed realized that she was trying to save his skin, and that he was very near to losing it. He held up his hands as if he'd just been arrested and backed slowly toward the screen door. Rasputin and Godiva sat down and eyed his retreat with regret.

Thena exhaled in relief. "I've hidden a component of the radio. You'll never find it, Jedidiah. And I've hidden the key to my boat. You can rage and roar, you can threaten me, but I'll never tell you where either thing is."

He anchored his hands on his lean hips. "Little lady, if you think you can rope and tie me this way, you've got another think comin'."

Thena calmly clasped her hands in front of her. "Get your gear and come back before dark or you'll get lost. I'll give you a beer and a plate of broiled sea trout, with homemade rolls. You'll be perfectly happy, once you relax. You can tell me all about Wyoming."

She had the feeling that she was the first person in years to provoke him this way. His jaw worked angrily as he glared at her. When he spoke, his voice seemed to have dropped at least one octave, which made it sound deadly.

"I'll live on the beach eatin' seaweed and turtle eggs before I'll roll over and play puppy for you," he informed her. "I'll flag down a boat."

"Good luck. Not many come by this way." She smiled, although she felt weak in the pit of her stomach. Thena had to give him credit for determination. That was something she admired deeply, even if it did make the situation much more difficult. "When you lose your desire to play Robinson Crusoe, there'll be a clean bed and good food waiting here for you."

"It'll be a cold day in hell."

"That's too bad. The next cold day here won't be until January."

He advanced again, stopped again at the dogs' fierce bristling, and jabbed one forefinger at her. "When I get my hands on you, I'll tie you to that big ol' bed of yours and let you watch while I tear this house apart. I'll find that radio part or the boat key."

"You're free to go anytime you want." She whipped a hand out in a gesture of airy dismissal. "Swim to the mainland." Tie her to the bed? Would he really stoop to a personal attack? she wondered breathlessly. And if he did, would he be a gentleman? Or could the term "gentleman" even be considered for someone who'd tie a woman to a bed?

"I could come back here," he began, "with my gun—"

"Pooh. You wouldn't really shoot me, and you know it. Stop talking like a cowboy, cowboy."

"What do you want from me, lady? You don't want my body, that's for sure. I got that message loud and clear."

He was so wrong. She loved his build and the way he moved, quiet and easy, but with power. He was the kind of man who wouldn't have to jostle his way through a crowd. He'd just amble between people, twisting those wide shoulders gracefully, always conscious of his movements but nonchalant about them. He was a man who thought of his body as a tool, not an ornament. She found that very appealing.

"I want your cooperation," Thena answered. "I want your attention—"

"Go swimmin' nekkid again sometime, and you'll get it," he challenged.

She covered her mouth in dismay and blushed

deeply. "You were here the other afternoon when I went swimming on the west shore?"

He was seething, and he wanted to provoke her. "Oh, yes, ma'am, and let me tell you, I can't remember when I've enjoyed a show more. You're a filly with mighty fine conformation. Good legs, trim ankles, a beautiful chest, a delicate neck, a strong back, and a solid rump. 'Course, it's too bad that you got a lame knee." He disliked that cruel choice of taunts immediately when he saw wounded bitterness touch her eyes. "But that doesn't matter, 'cause you're the kind of pretty filly a man would want to use for breedin', not workin'."

Thena looked down her nose at him. "Most men remind me of a particularly ugly variety of pig. And I'd say that you're king of pigs."

"I'd say there's somethin' funny about the way you acted when I smooched you today. I'd say that there for a minute you wanted to take a wild wallow with the ol' king of pigs here."

"What lovely analogies. What a lovely person you are. I usually have to go to a stockyard to meet a man of your quality. How thoughtful of you to bring such brilliant repartee to my island."

He held out both hands in angry supplication. "I don't want to be here. You don't want me here. There's a durned fantastic solution to this problem. You call ol' Farlo, I wait for him on that excuse-for-a-boat-dock you got, and he takes me far away from here, back where the gals talk sense and appreciate a good man."

"I appreciate a good man who appreciates the beauty of my island," she retorted. "And you're going to stay here until you do."

"I'll be deaf, dumb, blind, and senile by then."

"Which won't be much of a change, I'm sure."

In a battle of words, she would always win, Jed acknowledged glumly. "Dammit!" he said in frustration.

"What a marvelous vocabulary." She nodded politely to him and walked back down the hall to her studio. Thena heard the screen door slam and his heavy footsteps leave the porch. Her knees trembling, she sat down in a chair by her easel and debated her chances of changing his mind. He was certainly a roughneck cowboy, but she'd never met anyone with a more gallant heart. Thena realized suddenly that she had taken him prisoner for her sake, as well as the island's.

After she didn't see him for two days, her curiosity and a traitorous amount of worry for his survival goaded Thena to slip quietly among the beach pines and spy on him. She saw him standing in knee-deep waves, trying to fish with a long length of twine. He'd tied a handful of seashells to the twine as a sinker and created a makeshift hook somehow. He was a magnificent sight, shirtless, the legs of his jeans cut off a little above mid-thigh to reveal dark-haired legs molded by sinewy muscles.

She'd missed a great deal of normal human interaction, growing up on Sancia with reclusive scientists for parents, and having Jed here made her ache with regret for never learning the easy social aplomb so many mainland women seemed to possess. She'd just have to rely on what she'd seen in the movies. Now, if she were Marlene Dietrich in *Destry Rides Again*, she'd sidle up to Jed and purr, "Vee oughta be friends, you know, mister. Goood friends." And he'd do anything she wanted.

But she wasn't Marlene, and he wouldn't give in. If his fishing luck didn't change, he was going to starve. Thena hurried back through the forest, making plans.

The next morning Jed found a canvas bag in the sand next to the remnants of his campfire. So Miss Witch moved on silent feet, he thought. Not bad. For years he'd prided himself on the fact that his senses were so keen that no one could sneak up on him while he slept. "Probably a bomb," he muttered wryly, as he opened the bag.

But inside were rolls, fruit, homemade chocolate chip cookies, two big chunks of cheddar cheese, sunscreen lotion, fishing line, hooks and sinkers, a jug of spring water, and a note. The note said, "I'm not the enemy and you're not John Wayne. Please take a little help. Thena. P.S. Wouldn't you like a shave, an ice-cold beer, and a comfortable bed?"

Jed picked up each food item with loving care. He inhaled the aroma of the fruit and stared at the cookies a long time. Then he put everything back in the sack. Sighing, he sat cross-legged in the sand and rubbed a weary hand over the beard stubble that had turned his jaw into an itchy Brillo pad. Then he began to laugh. He loved this crafty woman. He loved her, but he wouldn't give in.

Thena found the sack on her front porch when she returned from the south marshes, where she'd gone to check on a nest of birds. She kicked her muddy walking shoes off and sat down by the bag. He hadn't taken a thing, not even the fishing gear, she discovered. What a man. What a tenacious, hard-headed, wonderful man. He was becoming very easy to adore.

Three more days passed. Thena began to grow edgy as the battle wore on her nerves and concentration. She never heard gunshots, so she knew he wasn't hunting the island game. He must be living on what few fish he could catch. And she knew that his only water supply was the slightly brackish creek that ran across his side of the island.

On the morning of the fourth day, she went to one of the inlets and gathered a few oysters for dinner. Rasputin and Godiva went with her, and as they neared the house on the way back, their ears perked up and they began to bark. Both big dogs bounded ahead, and Thena hurried after them. When she reached the porch, she halted, her mouth opened in alarm.

A haggard-looking Jed was stretched out on the rough plank floor, his ankles crossed and his head pillowed on his rolled-up sleeping bag. He wore nothing but his cutoffs and the old leather sandals she'd given him. He squinted at her for a moment, then raised one work-scarred hand and saluted. The gesture appeared to take effort.

"John Wayne surrenders," he murmured weakly. He put his hand down and closed his eyes.

"Oh, Jedidiah." Thena ran up the porch steps and sat down beside him. He had lost at least ten pounds off a frame that had been as lean as a runner's anyway. His face, neck, and arms, already bronzed by the Wyoming sun, were the only parts of him that the Georgia sun hadn't burned. The thick mat of hair on his chest was now more blond than brown, and a fine pattern of blisters ran across the tops of his shoulders. His jaw was covered in thick bristle, and he had new squint lines around his eyes. His lips had cracked from the constant beach wind.

"Go ahead and say it," he murmured, his eyes still shut. "I look like hell."

Thena disregarded common sense and patted his cheek tenderly. "L'homme magnifique," she whispered under her breath.

"What? Who's home?"

"The beard makes you look like that actor on *Miami Vice.*"

He smiled at that kind remark and looked up at her wearily. "Just give me something to fish with. I'm tired of trawlin' for minnows with my leg hairs."

"Why didn't you hunt? You could have killed a deer, or a rabbit."

"I figured you'd never forgive me if I blasted one of the inmates here at Eden," he grumbled.

"You mean you went hungry just so you wouldn't hurt my feelings?"

"Pa always said I was dumber than a rock."

Thena's eyes glistened with tears. Now she was certain she could change his mind about her island. He had a huge, soft heart that he could no longer keep hidden from her. She took his face between her graceful hands and looked deep into his eyes. Her mind very carefully ignored the surge of physical desire that made her tremble inside. She concentrated instead on a sweet sense that she could trust him, that she liked him more than she'd ever liked anyone in her life.

"What a cowboy," she whispered proudly. Then she leaned forward and brushed a gentle kiss across his forehead.

"Well . . . well damn." His voice was a low rumble. "If I'd known you were gonna act like this, I'd have surrendered three days ago."

Thena smiled wistfully and sat back. "Stay put," she ordered. She went inside. When she returned a few minutes later, she carried a glass of milk, a bunch of bananas, and a quart-sized coffee can. "Sit up and eat while I rub something on your shoulders."

He gulped the milk down and ate a banana before she even had time to kneel behind him and open the coffee can. "What is that stuff? Can I eat it? I could eat the hind leg off a mule, right now."

"You don't want to eat this. It's an herbal poultice that I keep in the refrigerator. My friend Beneba Everett made it."

"Huh. I've heard of her. Farlo Briggs says she taught you everything you know about bein' a witch. That stuff's gonna turn me into a frog, I bet."

"Farlo thinks she's a witch just because she grows the best garden in this part of the state. He's jealous."

"Aaaah. That's cold. It feels great. I won't mind bein' a frog."

He ate several more bananas while she smeared

the pasty concoction over his well-formed shoulders and back. He was too worn out and sunburned to be a threat, but still Thena felt uncomfortable touching him. His muscles bunched and relaxed under her fingertips, and she had to control the urge to massage the poultice in a little more than required. His skin was disturbingly hot from the sun.

When she finished, she handed him the coffee can. "You do the rest. I'll get you something else to eat."

"How 'bout a side of beef and a dozen of those ice-cold beers you kept temptin' me with?"

She laughed. "I get the idea."

He settled for two thick cheese omelets and a half pound of bacon. It seemed to her that he ate for hours. Plus, he drank two beers and two more glasses of milk with a gusto that made her want to cry.

"I'm so sorry you stayed out on the beach for five days," she blurted. "You're a very dauntless man."

"Yeah, the sun burned my 'daunt' off the first day."

She laughed, but sounded more upset than amused. "I'm really sorry," she emphasized.

He gulped down a last swallow of milk and smiled carefully so as not to hurt his mouth. With a milk mustache on his upper lip and his brown hair tousled, he looked like a teenager. "If you're really sorry, you'll finish rubbin' that cool goo on me. I haven't got any on the front of my legs, and they sting like crazy." He made himself look pitiful. "I'm so . . . so weak and kind of . . . woozy."

"Can the chatter and lie down, you cheap con artist."

"Where'd you learn such tough talk?" He stretched out slowly, and it seemed to Thena that every muscle in his stomach moved in a way calculated to draw her attention.

"Edward G. Robinson." She spread the ointment

on his feet, first. "Good heavens, Jedidiah, the membranes between your toes are red. Are you sunburned all over?"

"Will you put ointment everywhere, if I say yes?"

"We'll get along a great deal better if you don't flirt with me."

"You kissed me, wildflower. Right between the eyes. I'm allowed to flirt."

"That was a . . . friendly gesture. Sympathy from one human who admires another. . . ."

"Then explain to me where admirin' ends and lovin' begins."

Thena's fingers slipped awkwardly over his knees. She ignored his request. Love? This cowboy was pulling her leg. "Bony. Your knees are bony. And you have scars all over your legs." Oddly enough, they weren't unattractive to her. Oh, no, Thena thought. When you start to like somebody's little imperfections, then you're a goner. She cleared her throat roughly. "What did you do when you were growing up, sir? Play skip rope with barbed wire?"

She rubbed a little ointment on his thighs, feeling the long muscles quiver as she did. Thena plunked the can down. Breathing too fast, she scooted away from him and leaned her back against the side of the house. He rolled over on one side and locked her eyes in a serious, intense gaze.

"I grew up mean and I grew up fast," he told her. "I quit school in the tenth grade. My father was a drunk and he died in a knife fight. I've seen a lot of ugly things and I've done a few myself. But I'm honest, and I don't hurt anybody or anything unless they try to hurt me or someone I love. I don't drink much and I don't do drugs. I'm generous with what I've got, whether it's money or food or kindness." He paused, his eyes searching her face. "I know you and me are light years apart in some ways, but in others I feel like I've never been closer to another soul in my whole life."

Thena took a ragged breath. "You can be very eloquent when you want to be," she murmured. "Would you like a shave? Then I'll turn on the attic fan and you can go upstairs and take a nap."

"Are you tryin' to get me outta your hair?"

"Yes."

"Is it because of what I just told you about myself?"

"No. My parents taught me to judge a person by his actions and his nature, not by his past. I meant it last week when I said that I see the beauty in you. But . . . you want something from me that . . ."

"I wasn't hintin' that I wanted to spoon with you again," he teased softly. She cut her eyes at him in rebuke. "Well, okay, maybe I do want to spoon a little—"

"Please don't talk like that." Her voice broke on the last word. "Are you trying to ruin our friendship?"

"Are we friends, Thena?"

She nodded and sighed. "I'm afraid I can't help myself. We're friends. At least temporarily."

"Could it ever be more?"

She shook her head. "Not with you. Not with anyone." A tear slid down her cheek and she hurriedly brushed it away. She looked at him in despair. "Can we please just not discuss this subject again? Please?"

His mouth opened in protest, but he caught himself in time to hold his bewilderment and frustration inside. She must have loved that professor like life itself, Jed thought dully. And she's not over him yet. Patience, he told himself. She can be gentled. She can be won.

"You got it, wildflower." His voice was sincere. "I know you've been hurt. I can pretend to be a gentleman, when I have to. And I will. Relax."

"You are very much a gentleman, in all the ways that are important. You don't have to pretend."

"So I'm Jedidiah, not Jed, and a gentleman, not a rich saddle tramp. You're good for my ego, gal."

"You're good for me . . . because you're a challenge. I have so much to teach you about this island. You have to give me a chance."

The look in her eyes beseeched him in a way that made him feel he held the key to her happiness. A sense of protectiveness swelled up inside him, and at that moment he would have cheerfully fought dragons with his bare hands on her behalf. He figured this magical place probably had a few, puffing around somewhere.

"All right, gal. You keep feedin' me, and I swear I'll listen with an open mind."

Her face brightened. "I'll raise your consciousness yet."

He smiled at her wickedly. "Give it a chance to get over bein' sunburned, first."

Six

He slept all day. At dusk, Thena gave into an odd, restless impulse to see him and hear his voice. She tiptoed upstairs, found the door to the bedroom open, and peeked in furtively. It was too hot to keep the door closed. She expected that. She didn't expect to see his shorts and white briefs lying on the old plank floor or his lying naked on his stomach with his head burrowed in a pillow.

Stunned, Thena studied his relaxed body with an awe she usually reserved for magnificent sunrises. The sheets curled around him like a milky river, their pale softness a startling contrast to his hard angles and sun-baked skin. Of course he's not sunburned everywhere, she thought blankly, staring at the smooth white skin on his rump.

Thena tilted her head to one side and looked at it with an artist's eye. How lovely and symmetrical it was. Her academic nature noted the well-toned appearance of the muscles. Yes, the gluteals—maximus, medius, and minimus—were in excellent shape. Quite excellent. Quite appealing and vulnerable. Quite touchable, really, and her fingertips were very interested in proving it.

Aghast, Thena tiptoed away, went downstairs, and curled up in an overstuffed chair with comfortably sprung springs. The summer twilight and the island's night sounds slipped inside and surrounded her. Thena sat in the dark a long time, trying to decide at what point her chemical reactions to Jed Powers had gotten totally out of control.

Her father had been taller than Jed, but not much bigger around. Thena went into a back storage room, where she unpacked a pair of blousey white work pants and rolled up the legs. She also aired out one of the faded Hawaiian shirts her father had adored. Tom Selleck attire it was not, but at least Jed would be adequately covered. Getting him covered was a crucial project to her.

At ten o'clock he ambled downstairs, the denim cutoffs slung low on his hips. Seated in her chair again, a floor lamp creating a pool of light around her, Thena looked up from her latest sojourn through the world of *Oliver Twist*. The dogs, stretched out on the floor near her feet, watched Jed with growing acceptance. They only growled once.

"Bathroom," he mumbled sleepily.

Her face taut with the effort of not staring at the descending V of hair on his stomach, she pointed down the hall. He smiled at her and started toward it.

"There are fresh clothes in there for you."

"Thanks. What're you readin'?" he asked over his shoulder.

"Charles Dickens. My favorite."

"I remember him. Wrote about England. Hmmmm, *David Copperfield*. Only book I didn't fall asleep over in class." Thena stared at him in pleased surprise, her lips parted.

"I'm reading *Oliver Twist*."

"Has it got a few laughs in it?"

"A few."

"Will you read some of it to me after I take a shower?"

"Well . . . certainly. I'll fix something to eat, if you're hungry. How do you like hot dogs?"

"By the dozen."

Hot dogs and Dickens. They spent several hours indulging in both. The warm, fragrant night air sifted through the screen door and the open windows. The tame hawk Jed had seen the first day landed outside the door and delicately ate morsels of canned tuna that Thena left in a bowl for it. Thena sat in the easy chair and Jed lay down on the couch nearby. The room was lit only by the floor lamp.

Jed listened to *Oliver Twist* with sincere interest, his eyes dark with intrigue. Thena felt them on her, never moving, as still as the shadows that pooled in the corners of the house. When an ancient grandfather clock next to the television chimed twice, Thena put her book down and looked at it in surprise. She'd been reading to Jed for several hours.

"Not a bad story. Makes me wish I'd read more good books when I had the chance. I'd like to hear the rest, and you got a pretty voice. How about tomorrow?"

"Are you serious?"

"Damn pretty. You sort of sing when you talk—"

"I meant, are you serious about Dickens? About *Oliver Twist*?" Flustered and secretly pleased, Thena nearly dropped her book. And not because he was interested in literature.

"Yep. I feel content to be still and listen." He blinked languidly. "You know what? If I hadn't nearly turned into a french fry on your beach, I would have enjoyed livin' there. I can see why people like the ocean. It makes you feel peaceful."

"See? You're learning to appreciate Sancia already. Would you like to go back to SalHaven tomorrow?"

"Nope. I'll go anywhere but there."

"All right. Then you can follow me around."

"Now that's a right interestin' idea—"

"And count crabs."

He clasped his chest dramatically. "She shot him down bad, right through the heart."

Thena chuckled. "I count sand crabs regularly.

Over the years, my records might reveal dramatic changes in their population. That could be important to everything they eat, and everything that eats them."

"I'll eat them unless you get me another hot dog." They shared a companionable laugh.

Companionable. That was the perfect way to describe the relationship that developed between them during the next few days, Thena decided. He seemed to relish her talkative, animated presence, and in return, she enjoyed his unhurried attitude. He didn't indulge in moods. He was solid and quiet, calm to the point that a stranger might have thought him completely indifferent to everything around him.

But she was no stranger—sometimes a poignant, puzzling sense of closeness made her feel that he and she had never really been strangers—and Thena knew that under his facade lay an intensely observant nature. Because she was often the recipient of both the disturbing intensity and the observation, she never mistook his nonchalance for indifference.

Thena talked carefully about SalHaven, mentioning innocuous facts that left his grandfather Gregg out of the conversation. The "Sal" came from his grandmother Sarah's nickname, Sally, she told Jed. The old-timers on the mainland had never forgotten her kindness, her lack of snobbishness, and her charity work. A tall, athletic woman with auburn hair, she rode her beloved Arabians with incomparable grace.

"I've seen pictures of her," Thena said. "You have her eyes."

"Is that good?" Jed asked in his slow, teasing way. "What do my eyes look like?" Everything he did and said seemed to have a sensuous undertone, or else her chemicals had infiltrated her imagination and were making it work overtime, Thena decided.

"You have very intelligent eyes." She paused slyly. "But then, so does a wild goat."

They were sitting in rocking chairs on the front porch, having just returned from counting loggerhead turtle nests on the beach. Jed's wet, dirty sandals lay near his feet. In one easy motion, he scooped a sandal up and lobbed it into her lap. It spattered grit and water on her white shorts. In the lighthearted battle that followed, she chased him into the front yard, her own dirty sandal raised to throw.

He stubbed his big toe on a cactus plant and, true to his nature, didn't make a sound. Instead, he grinned nonchalantly and limped with haste to the safety of her big water cistern. He climbed the ten-rung ladder that ran up one side and hoisted himself over the barrel top. Thena heard a splash as he disappeared from sight. This was childish and absurd, but she couldn't remember when she'd had a better time.

"You're not safe from me up there!" she yelled.

"Good! Come and get me, gal!"

"All right!"

She ran to the ladder and climbed hurriedly while he splashed over to the far side of the cistern, whooping with great feigned fear. When she reached the top and swung herself over the side, he yelled, "We've been boarded by lady Klingons, Captain! Run for your life, Spock! I'll rassle the little thing to a standstill and take her to the brig!"

"What's a Klingon?" she asked breathlessly, just as he dove underwater and grabbed her ankles. Thena gasped as he pulled her under with him. They wrestled playfully for a minute and popped above the surface together, laughing. She was in his arms.

"What's a Klingon?" he echoed in amazement, gazing down at her. Then his eyes turned comically shifty. "It's a love-starved critter that can't keep its paws off cowboys." Then he kissed her full on the mouth and let her go. He went back to his side of the cistern.

"Oh . . . oh! Sorry I asked!" Perturbed and tingling, she splashed over to her side and clung to it, desperately. Thena turned her back to him and rested her head on her arms, frowning. "I'm not a Klingon," she told him in a firm tone.

"Well, let's just test you out and see if you're tellin' the truth."

She heard soft sloshing sounds, and the water in the cistern undulated as if he were moving about. Thena refused to look at him, determined not to encourage his antics. Seconds later, something soggy smacked the cistern wall near her. She jumped and looked quickly to her right. Her father's shirt and pants—Jed's shirt and pants—hung over the old wood siding.

"Turn around, lady Klingon," Jed ordered in a low, gruff voice. "Or are you chicken?"

Thena took a deep breath and pivoted about, then plastered her back to the cistern wall. Jed waited on the other side, his magnificent torso bare, the water lapping sensuously at a level that teased her by revealing his navel, then hiding it, then showing it again, then hiding it. . . .

Thena quickly pulled her gaze upward. He smiled coyly, but his eyes glinted with something serious and provocative. "Watch now, Klingon," he drawled in a throaty voice. "See if you can resist."

He began to cup water over his naked chest, spreading his hands wide and making long, slow strokes from his collarbone all the way to that disturbing navel. Up, down, up, down, slower and slower. She was hypnotized. His thick brown chest hair followed the patterns he caressed on his pectoral muscles, and she was close enough to see the goose bumps on his nipples. He presented a glistening picture of male temptation. His arms and shoulders were corded with muscle, and his waist tapered cleanly into the water. She could imagine exactly what the submerged parts of him looked like.

"Come on over here, Klingon." His voice was just a whisper. "You come over here and do this for me. And then I'll do it for you. I know how you Klingons love to have your chests stroked."

Thena fought for a semblance of calm. Her skin felt so hot that she wondered why the water didn't steam around her. There wasn't enough water in the world to fight the sweet fire low in her body.

"I've still got my drawers on," Jed purred. "I'm decent."

"Jedidiah, you're not very subtle at seduction."

"Maybe you want to be seduced and I don't have to be subtle." He smiled as if he were teasing, but his intense, compelling eyes were ordering her to strip naked so that his hands could roam over her body.

She lifted her chin primly. "I don't approve of this game. I'm going back in the house." She turned and climbed over the side of the cistern, then went down the ladder without giving him a second glance. She marched across the yard.

"Reckon I'll come with you," he called cheerfully. Thena swung around and watched as he hoisted himself out of the cistern and began climbing down. She took several steps backward, her eyes wide. He might as well have been naked. The cotton briefs clung to outlines that none of her biology books could do justice to, not even in a hundred color plates, she thought blankly.

He arched one brow at her, ran a thumb under his waistband, snapped it loudly against the taut, wet skin of his abdomen, and strolled—no, preened— toward her. She could think of only one way to diffuse the mixture of temptation and amusement in his eyes.

"And here's Monsieur Jedidiah on the runway," Thena deadpanned in a loud, dramatic voice, "show- ing us the newest in Paris fashions for the success- ful cowboy, or, as we say in the fashion business, 'el gay caballero.' Notice the simple but elegant cut of the design, the racing stripes, the wide elastic trim guaranteed to leave no panty line even under the tightest chaps."

"Aw, you're mean," he said drolly as he passed her. "And I was gonna let you rub some of that cold goo on my poor ol' sunburned belly." He tsked-tsked regretfully. "But you hurt my feelin's, so I'll just cut you short on thrills today."

"However will I manage?"

"Don't know." He continued to the porch, his hips flexing under the translucent cotton briefs, his back straight, his devastating show very effective indeed. "How did you get to the ripe age of twenty-five without ever seein' a nearly nekkid man?"

"Ah, so you're an amateur mind reader. What makes you mistakenly believe the sight of so much hairy and sunburned masculine skin is new to me?"

He walked up the porch steps, turned around, grinned lazily, and winked. "That baby black snake you ain't even noticed crawlin' across your right foot."

Thena jumped wildly when she realized that something was definitely tickling her toes. The harmless little snake dropped off her foot and wiggled faster, trying to get out of the way of such a leaping monster. Thena bent down and scooped him into one hand, then stood and glared at Jed. But deep down, she felt the beginnings of delighted laughter.

"You'll have a clammy, cold bed partner tonight," she promised fiendishly.

"Thanks for the offer, but I'll take the snake instead."

Laughing heartily, he turned and went through the screen door, slapping it shut behind him with a boisterous motion of one hand. Thena looked after him in bittersweet silence. She wished openly and desperately that she were the kind of woman who could make a man like Jed happy. She'd never wanted to reach out to someone so much in her life. The results, if she did, would almost certainly be embarrassing.

Thena bent her head over the slender black snake cupped in her hand. "He was joking, but you'd be sexier than me, little friend," she whispered sadly.

Jed cheerfully helped her explore the beaches for unusual shells. He learned to throw a fishnet, and in return, he taught her how to palm coins and play poker. Regardless of his coy remarks and blatant sensuality, he never touched her or tried to kiss her again. He didn't have to. Just being near him, just looking at him or listening to his deep, rumbling voice tell rodeo stories was enough to keep her flushed and a little short of breath.

One night he listened restlessly as she read *Call of the Wild*. When the clock signaled that three A.M. had arrived, and Thena's voice began to get hoarse, she held the book out to him. He lay on a braided rug near her bare feet, his muscular chest too bare, the outline of his legs and hips too provocative in her father's old white beach pants. She noticed that he was drumming his fingers on the rug, the gesture impatient.

"Here, Jedidiah, you read *Call of the Wild* out loud for a while."

He shoved his cocoa-brown hair back and muttered, "Tell me about your professor. What did you read to him?"

"Oh, Shakespeare, philosophy, esoteric French novels. Why?"

"Just wonderin'." He was silent for a moment, looking disgruntled for reasons she didn't understand.

"You've acted odd ever since I opened this book. Are you bored?" she asked.

"Nope." He stretched out on his back, put his hands under his head, and stared fixedly at the ceiling. Thena admired the rise and fall of his deep chest, until she saw that its movement was a little constricted. He was definitely tense about something. "Read some more. I like doggie books," he said drolly. "See Spot run."

Thena's mouth popped open. "Do you think I'm making fun of you?" she asked in amazement. "If I wanted to make fun of you, I'd read *Grimm's Fairy Tales for Six- to Eight-Year-Olds*. And explain the complicated parts."

"Guess your professor spouted about a dozen different languages."

"Well, yes, so what?"

"I speak some Spanish. Picked it up rodeoing in the Southwest."

"That's nice. *Bueno*."

"I'm gonna get my high school degree some day. I'm not illiterate or anything."

"*Bueno*." He cut his eyes at her, and she smiled quizzically. "What's this all about, Jedidiah?"

"I know plenty about animals—I could almost be a veterinarian. And I know about building houses. I could build one from the ground up, put in the wiring and the plumbing, do everything. And there's not a truck on the road that I couldn't fix, if it broke down. Most cars, too." He turned on his side and braced himself on one elbow, studying her intensely. "I read a lot of magazines—good stuff, like *Newsweek* and *Life*. None of those grocery store gossip sheets about aliens and Vanna White."

"Who's Vanna White?"

He thumped the floor with one fist, startling her and making the dogs growl from their spots on the porch. "Never mind about Vanna White. Dammit, you know what I'm gettin' at. I'm as smart as any man you've ever known, and I expect you to treat me that way."

Thena's mouth opened in shock as she realized that all his strange verbal meandering was meant to hide the fact that he was jealous of Nate. This tough man, who had punched his way out of innumerable brawls, made a living against tough odds, cared for an irresponsible father, and had still managed to turn out gallant, kind, and sensitive, thought she was a snob.

"Jedidiah Powers," she declared hotly, "I happen to think you're very intelligent. I happen to admire your determination and common sense. I happen to think that you're fine just the way you are."

His anger faded. He looked up at her with one eye squinted in a way that told her that he might smile eventually. "But could you love a man who never graduated from high school?"

Oh, no, she wasn't going to be drawn into that area of discussion. Thena clasped her hands to her head in a grand show of disbelief. "How did you develop this fixation on formal education?"

"From college gals who only wanted to date me behind their daddies' backs," he retorted. "I was good enough for a few kicks, but I wasn't good enough to take home to the folks. I made good grades in high school, but I had to drop out and go to work because of money problems. But that didn't matter to those gals."

"Mainland women are crazy, Jedidiah." She wasn't joking. Her face was so solemn that he looked at her askance and unexpected humor began to tickle his ribs. "They don't know what's important. I don't care if you graduated from high school or not."

"Well, what do you think's important, Miss Witch?"

Thena sighed and rubbed her head wearily. "I think it's important that I get a cup of hot tea and start reading this book again, so you'll be quiet." She looked at him sternly. "Decency, compassion, and courage are important. Having an open mind is important. Being capable of deep, unselfish love is important."

He propped his head on one hand, and his eyes

seemed to burn her skin. "I know I got that last part down," he murmured. "I know how to love that way." He paused. "Do you?"

Flustered, Thena opened her book again. "I hope so," she answered finally. She cleared her throat. "New chapter. Now, as you recall—"

"Calm down. Whoa." He got up slowly, his eyes never leaving her face. She knew he was searching her expression for answers, for promises, for hope. Thena tried to look impassive. "I'll get to you, gal," he said softly. She gazed at him wide-eyed. "I'll win you."

Her mouth opened, but no words came out. She couldn't honestly say she didn't want him to try, but she couldn't encourage him either. He just didn't understand that she was an intellectual creature with no talent for romance. Jed stepped forward, chucked her under the chin, and winked. "I'll make you some tea," he said. "You look like you could use it."

The next day he sat on the beach beside her and watched her paint. With the blunt sincerity of a man who didn't know art but knew what he liked, he dubbed her seascape, "Good, because it's real lookin'." His down-home charm and innate honesty were powerful attractions, and Thena began to worry that her constant smile might alert him to the giddy devotion that had begun to wreak havoc with her.

The lovely mood between them obscured the fact that he was still on the island against his will. He lay stretched out on the porch one afternoon, fiddling with a rope he'd gotten from the barn. Thena worked at the base of the porch, planting a row of mint in a small area she intended for an herb garden.

"I suppose I should let you go back to the mainland, if you want to," she ventured. "You've been living with me for five days." She kept her head down and dug diligently with a small spade. "And I don't think you've changed your mind about Sancia at all."

He was on the verge of changing, but he wasn't going to admit it yet. The place was getting to him. Its resident witch was getting to him. He kept thinking about marriage and babies, babies with silver eyes and dark brunet hair. "Reckon you want me to go," he mumbled.

"I know you must have business to take care of. . . ."

"Bought some mares, but they're bein' boarded because I don't have a ranch yet. Got no home, just a hotel room in Cheyenne. Got an expensive attorney with three names and a number—Chester Porter Thompson, the fourth—who looks after my interests. Nope. I got no business to take care of right away. Hey, I'm rich, remember. That means I can do whatever I want."

"Then I don't want you to go," she said frankly.

"Then I don't want to go," he answered just as frankly.

"Good."

"Fine."

They were both silent, and both continued concentrating on their respective activities. She glanced. He glanced. They both began to chuckle. "Get up," he ordered, and sat up himself. "I'm gonna teach you to throw a lasso."

Thena stood, gazing uncertainly at the rope he held between his skilled, brawny hands. He slid a neat, loose loop up and down it. She nodded down at her cutoff jeans and her voluminous, faded Hawaiian shirt.

"Do I look like a cowgirl?"

Jed wore a similar outfit—more clothes of her father's—and the fact that he and she matched had been a source of teasing this morning at breakfast. He'd accused her of wanting them to look like a pair of Miami tourists. He grinned.

"It ain't how you look, it's a state of mind. You got cowgirl written all over you."

"I can only assume that's a compliment."

"Yes, ma'am," he promised happily. He padded down the steps and motioned for her to follow him across the yard. "Tell that hunk of dog to go pose for practice," he instructed, nodding toward Rasputin, who lay beside Godiva on the porch.

"Rasputin, go." She pointed, and Rasputin, tongue lolling and eyes slitty as he scrutinized Jed and the rope, made his lazy way to a spot in the sandy yard. He flopped down. "Stay." She turned to Jed. "This isn't the kind of doggie that cowboys are supposed to rope."

"Woman, you're too much of a perfectionist." He stepped away, the noose growing larger in his nimble fingers. "This is called buildin' a loop." He swung it overhead and twirled it a few times, his easy grace an impressive sight. The loop sailed out and landed around Rasputin's thick neck. Jed pulled it snug without hurting the startled dog. "This," he said dryly, "is called revenge for all the times that critter growled at me." His voice rose dramatically. "Get the brandin' iron!"

"Oh, poor baby," Thena crooned, running to Rasputin and lifting the noose off him. The huge dog gave her a soulful, wounded look. "You be still. We're not going to hurt you."

"Get the fire hotter!" Jed called to some invisible accomplice. "Make that iron sizzle!"

"Ssssh." She stalked back to him, shaking her finger and smiling crookedly. "Let me try."

He sidled around behind her, and she felt every inch of her skin pull tight as his hands slid down her wrists. So this was his tactic, she thought anxiously. The old touch-and-snuggle method of lasso instruction.

"Now hold it easy," he drawled softly, as he guided her fingers into position on the rope. His breath was warm and fragrant against her neck. Warm and fragrant and a tad faster than normal. "Don't hold too tight, or it might not do what you want." Is he talking about the rope? She suspected not. "Don't hold too loose, or it'll get away from you and cause trouble. That's it . . . curl those fingers around it. Shake it a little, to get it ready."

"Now," she said sharply, "I swing it over my head and throw it away."

"Ooooh, ouch, no, don't even talk like that. This is an art."

"This is a sham."

"Nope, it's a lariat." He ran his fingers up her bare arms as he stepped back. "Go ahead. Swing it."

She was so perturbed by his teasing and the tickling warmth that had invaded her body that she swung too close to her head and let the loop get too big. Thena gasped as an immovable object stopped her twirling in mid-twirl. The loop had caught Jed, who stood about a foot behind her, around the neck.

"Mercy, ma'am!" he chortled. "I'll come along peaceably. Just be gentle when you break me." He stepped close to her and molded both hands to her waist, the pressure snug and squeezing. "Break me, Thena," he whispered in her ear. "Take me apart and put me back together again. You've got the power to do it."

His hands slid up the soft cotton shirt and cupped her breasts. Her knees went weak with the incredible, foreign sensation of a man's hands, Jed's hands, touching that part of her body. His fingers moved in an erotic massage, deliciously rough and intimate over the aroused peaks they found. "We both expected this. It's time we made love, Thena."

Thena groaned in despair and whipped around. She dropped the lariat and pushed him away with both hands, feeling reckless, her breath labored, her eyes gleaming with antagonism and frustration. He provoked her to primal sexual reactions; he wouldn't quit flirting; he courted disaster and had dredged up all her old longings as well as her old sense of inadequacy.

"I am not interested in these adolescent games!" she said angrily.

He looked at her in absolute amazement and then frowned. "We're not kids and this isn't a game. I'm not tryin' to take what I can get and then go my own way. When I said 'make love,' that's what I meant. If you can't see that I'm in love with you, then you're not lookin' very hard."

"Jedidiah, you don't really know me. Don't bandy an important word such as love—"

His hand snapped out and captured her wrist. She found herself staring into his hurt, fierce gaze. "Don't talk to me like I'm some kid who's got his first crush, dammit. I never said 'I love you' to anyone before."

"Well, don't say it to me!" Her voice broke on the last word and she tugged her wrist away. Her chest ached with the conflict his announcement caused. Love. This rough-cut cowboy loved her . . . and it would be foolish to deny that she loved him too. But she wouldn't let love become making love and ruin everything. Thena took several calming breaths. "I told you before, I don't want anything to do with you or any other man."

He ran a hand through his hair and shook his head in bewilderment. He couldn't understand how she could deny the incredible attraction between them. Jed forced his voice to relax. "Hey, Miss Witch, if you really feel that way, why do you want me to stay here?"

"You're not . . . not ready to leave. You still don't understand why this island is worth preserving."

"You know, I don't take to bein' forced to do things. This isn't funny anymore. Now, look, I've been a good sport for the past few days. If my touch makes you so uncomfortable"—he paused, struggling not to sound as upset as he felt—"then I want you to get on the radio and—"

"Not until you agree to leave my island alone."

"It ain't your island!"

"We're back where we started with this argument," she said stiffly. "I'm going to the beach and paint for a while. Good-bye." Thena turned on one heel and walked away, her back rigid. Jed watched her go, his confusion over her attitude growing into an anger that ate at his patience. Something had to give.

Seven

His growing restlessness over Thena's strange behavior and a bad night's sleep made tension coil inside Jed like a snake waiting to strike. He came downstairs barefoot, cursing the floppy white pants with their drawstring waist and the gaudy shirt that he hadn't yet buttoned. He had to get off this island before Thena turned him into some sort of goofy-looking beachcomber who was too addled to keep his plans straight.

She wouldn't let him leave, but she wouldn't admit that she had motives for keeping him here other than the preservation of her island. He saw the sexual interest in her eyes, dammit; he read it in the languid, appealing way she moved when she was around him. On that count, at least, he knew she cared about him. Her aloofness was maddening, but the sadness that lay under it aroused the protective part of his nature. Her mystery could drive a man to total adoration and total insanity at the same time.

Last night they'd sat in rigid silence and watched a tape of an old Lassie movie. She cried quietly during the sad parts, which seemed to come about every five minutes. He decided that she was crying over a lot more than a collie dog, so he sat down on the floor beside her chair and offered her his quiet sympathy and devotion. That made her cry harder and abruptly go to her bedroom. She shut the door and never came back.

Jed stopped at the bottom of the stairs, his face set in stoical lines. He wasn't stupid. She liked him, sure, but she wasn't interested in lovin' a simple horse wrangler.

Suddenly he heard the soft melody of her voice as it whispered out of her bedroom. "Appreciate," he heard dimly. "Groceries . . . thanks, Grandmother. Good-bye." He inched close to the open door and peeked in. Her back to him, Thena slipped something small out of her ham radio. Jed's eyes narrowed as she brushed her long hair out of the way and fiddled with the buttons down the front of her old-fashioned white chemise. When she finished, her hands were empty. So that's where she was hiding things.

"Gimme that radio part," he ordered tersely. "Or hand over the boat key."

She whirled around, her gray eyes wide with shock. "Get away from my door, you spy!"

He stepped inside the room, his hands clenched. "Give me the damn boat key."

"You arrogant rooster. Rasputin! Godiva!"

"Oh, no, you don't." He slammed the bedroom door and strode over to the window that opened onto the porch. A dozen tiny wrens fluttered away from the birdseed on the sill as Jed jerked the bottom of the window down. He turned on Thena and advanced with measured, tensed steps. She retreated to the other side of her bed and glared at him through the gauze of white mosquito netting that flowed from the ceiling over it.

"Assault and battery," she warned.

"Kidnappin'," he reminded her. "We'll be even. Give me the boat key."

He'd taught her a few cowboy phrases, Now she used one. "Brand me and break me, but I'll still bite."

Unperturbed, he flung himself across the bed with a speed that caught her by surprise. Thena stumbled back, but he grabbed her by one arm. Off balance she was no match for his maneuver, and he pulled her roughly toward him. Thena collapsed on the bed in a heap of sheets and mosquito netting, hugged her free arm over her chest protectively, and curled up in a defensive ball against his thigh.

"*Sacrebleu!*" she yelled fiercely. "No!"

"I don't like doin' this," he growled, as he wound his fingers into the back of her chemise. He emphasized every word in a last-chance, threatening tone as his grip tightened. "Give—me—the—boat—key."

"When turtles fly!"

Everything happened with mind-boggling quickness. He ripped the chemise down the back from neckline to hem. Thena flailed wildly as she felt cool morning air on the length of her body. She'd never expected him to strip her. As usual, she wore no underwear.

"Jedidiah, don't!"

"Give me that damn key or I'll leave you buck nekkid!"

"No!" She pushed herself upright and tried to scramble away, both arms crossed over her chest. He grabbed the front hem of her chemise and Thena gasped as it tore up the middle all the way to her full breasts. Defeated, embarrassed, and furious, Thena flung the remnants of it, with the key and the radio part pinned to the bodice, at him.

"There!" she cried bitterly. "Take the boat key! Go back to the mainland, if that's all you can think about doing! I'll be glad to get rid of your provocative, primitive presence!"

Jed forgot the torn garment that lay in his lap. Thena, her breasts and face flushed, her legs curled under her, was a golden, naked wildcat with tangled brunette hair. The most infuriating, the most unattainable, and the most desirable woman he'd ever known sat not more than a foot away from him, making no attempt to cover herself, almost daring him to stare at what his violent behavior had accomplished.

He understood why when he noticed the glistening, fierce pride in her eyes, pride so unyielding that it wouldn't let her give into the other emotions he saw—the vulnerability and embarrassment. She was a mesmerizing sight that stabbed at his heart and charged him with regret.

"Look at me!" she ordered, her whole body trembling. "I won't hide! I'm not beaten!" He watched her eyes fill with tears of pure frustration. "Why did you have to come to my island? Why didn't you just sell it and send your developers instead! I could have fought them, but you . . . you don't fight fairly." Tears streaked her face as she glanced down at her nakedness. "Get out! Go away."

"Hush, sssh," he crooned suddenly. Jed grabbed a sheet and pulled it around her shoulders.

She was so surprised that her tears stopped. She sat as still as a statue as he covered her up, his expression making her ache with absurd sorrow for upsetting him. That didn't make sense, she told herself. He'd upset her. She was getting confused. A strange current flowed from him, bewildering her with its mixture of desire, affection, and anguish.

"Come here, Miss Witch," Jed said in a gruff, kind voice.

"You've gotten what you wanted. You don't have to debase yourself with an apology."

"God, woman, just because you know how to talk real well, you don't have to talk all the time. Be quiet."

He slid close to her on the bed and pulled her to him for a gentle hug. Thena made a strangled, bittersweet sound when his hand guided her head to his warm shoulder. After a tense moment she let it rest there. His shirt was askew, and her cheek tingled at the contact with his skin and hard, sheathed muscles.

"Ask me to stay in your bed, you proud little filly," he told her, every word hoarse. "Tell me that some of the reasons you want me here don't have anything to do with this island."

Instead of answering, Thena did something she'd been wanting to do for days. The angry, reckless atmosphere jumbling her thoughts, she tilted her face up a little and kissed his cheek, letting her lips linger against the coarse skin and faint shadow of morning beard.

Jed groaned softly and twisted his head so that his mouth came down on hers. Startled, Thena went absolutely still as his lips tantalized and tugged, sending warmth throughout her body. She felt as if she were being drawn under by a tumultuous ocean wave, that sensations were overwhelming her with an elemental force as old as time. Eager to please, desperate to hide her lack of experience, she copied the response she'd seen actresses give in the old movies. She made her face impassive and didn't move her mouth a fraction.

"Kiss me back," Jed urged, his voice sad. "Please, kiss me back, Thena."

Nervous and awkward, Thena tensed her mouth and ground it into Jed's, hard. She wanted him to stay forever.

After a moment he pulled away, frowning. The dark distress in his eyes alarmed her. "All right, you don't have to fake it," he muttered. "If you don't want to kiss me, don't pretend. I'd get more response kissing a brick wall."

"Do you . . . what do you want me to do?" she asked, as a rivulet of humiliation wound around her stomach.

"Just act like a woman who wants to love a man. Me."

He didn't understand that she wanted that more than anything. Thena felt a painful twist of undeniable truth. She just couldn't make love to Jed, no matter how much she wanted to. It would be a disaster, a disappointment that would shame her and make him lose interest. Nate had predicted this failure, she thought dully. Attraction comes from an inner wellspring of sensuality, he'd told her often. Some people don't have it. Her spring must be dry.

Desperate, Thena cleared her throat and gave Jed a firm look. She'd try one more time to show that she wanted to love him in body as well as spirit. "I'll be happy to touch you." She pointed to the front of his pants. "There."

He nearly choked on frustration. "No, thanks. I had somethin' a lot more important than a quick thrill in mind. And you know it."

Her voice rose with anguish. "Jedidiah, I can't satisfy you if you're going to be choosy about what kind of thrill you'll accept."

He got up off the bed, taking the chemise with him. Jed unpinnned the boat key and threw the tattered material on the floor. His eyes glittered with anger. "I reckon this sounds pretty funny, comin' from somebody like me . . . but I'm interested in love. You're interested in sex." Jed paused. "And you're pretty damn odd about the whole business."

Odd. Her hopes sank. Yes, she was odd and purely intellectual, and she shouldn't try to be anything else. Thena pulled her sheet closer around her. Even though it was July, she felt cold. Cold and alone and ancient. "It was nice having you here," she said in a low, polite voice. "Leave the boat at the Dundee municipal docks. I'll have someone bring it back."

"Is that all you can say to me?" he asked. Their eyes met. His were searching and hard. "Aren't you willing to admit that there's something damn fantastic and special between us? Won't you warm up to me just a little?"

She looked at him very calmly. "You're male, I'm female. That fact gave rise to some inevitable hormonal interplay. That sums up our relationship nicely. I'll have someone bring the boat back," Thena repeated. "You'd better go right away. My neighbor, Beneba, says a thunderstorm's coming." She paused. "I suppose I'll see you in court, about the island."

Jed looked at her in stunned silence. Then he shook his head. "I reckon you belong out here, all alone. It suits you."

Thena couldn't trust her voice to answer that cruel comment, so she simply nodded. He left the room. She stayed on the bed, listening wretchedly as he quickly gathered his things and walked out the front door without saying good-bye. And Thena, who had always loved being by herself, cried because now she could hardly stand the emptiness he left behind.

The August sun burned a round hole in the sky directly over Thena's head. Its rays seeped through her wide-brimmed straw hat, making a kaleidoscope of shadows on her drawing pad and the hypnotizing masculine face coming to life under her pencil.

She dug her toes in the sand and shifted a little, the beach feeling scratchy even through her shorts. That was the only distraction she allowed in her pursuit of the perfect likeness of Jed. She tuned out the gulls crying overhead, the rushing sound of the waves licking the tide line, and the steady whisper of the ocean breeze.

She'd drawn dozens of pictures of the Wyoming cowboy who'd left her emotions in such disarray a month ago. Instead of fading with time, her mental images of him grew more detailed. She drew him on horseback; she drew him looking squinty-eyed and sexy like Clint Eastwood; she drew him naked, using her imagination to fill in the parts she'd never seen. She drew him, and she missed him more each time she finished.

The distant sound of Rasputin's and Godiva's ferocious barking made her leap up. Thena ran toward the warning, her heart hammering because it came from the west, where Sancia's tiny old dock was located. She realized that she was going to spend the rest of her life hoping that Jed would come back.

Cendrillon and the dogs met her halfway to the dock. Thena tucked her drawing pad under one arm, then swung up on the mare's back, and the four of them continued together. A few yards from the dock Thena stopped Cendrillon with a voice command. She removed the dark sunglasses she always wore on the beach and stared at the sleek cabin cruiser bellying up to her dock like a bloated whale.

Four clean-cut men, dressed in fashionable hiking clothes and carrying everything from backpacks to camera bags and rifles, tromped down the rickety dock toward her. Only Thena's most curt commands kept Rasputin and Godiva from crouching for an attack.

"You must be the caretaker's granddaughter," called one of the men, a portly executive type who looked lost without his desk and secretary.

"This is a private island," she said in a formal voice. "State your business."

The man pulled a card from the vest pocket of his well-pressed khaki safari shirt. He started forward, was met by the dogs' low growls, and stopped tentatively.

"I can't have your animals endangering my group," he informed her stiffly.

"I can't have your group endangering my animals. Who are you?"

"We're from Baylor-Michaels-Sutton. Developers."

Disbelief and anger zinged through Thena's veins. "Has the island been sold?"

"Not yet. We're prospective buyers." His eyes, under a ridiculous-looking golf hat, assessed Cendrillon. "Is this one of the wild horses that comes with the place?"

Horror sent a chill down Thena's back. Had she wounded Jed's ego so much that he'd take this kind of revenge? No, she trusted his goodness too much to believe he'd sell her horses, especially Cendrillon. "None of the horses come with 'this place,' " she answered in a freezing voice.

"I'm afraid the owner's attorney says everything is included except the caretaker's house and five acres around it. Animal populations, the old Gregg mansion, everything. We hope you'll show us around. We want to do a little hunting while we're here."

Thena winced at his last remark and gave Cendrillon a silent signal, and the mare began backing away. "Let me go to the house and put on my hiking shoes," she called sweetly, "and I'll be glad to play guide."

"Terrific! We'll look for a campsite."

Smiling, nodding, Thena swung Cendrillon around and nudged her into a fast lope, the dogs racing alongside. Find a campsite, my unsuspecting little visitors, she thought grimly. Rest. You'll need all your energy before I'm finished with you. Jed had sent them, and his betrayal spurred her to bitter action.

"Twenty-five," Jed said lazily, leaning on the corral fence as he studied the prize-winning quarter horse mare. He wanted this horse badly, but as with most things he wanted, he knew how to appear nonchalant. "Yep. Let me have Miss Kitty Can Do for twenty-five thousand and I'll pay whatever you want to board her until I find myself a ranch."

Beyond the mare's sleek body, the rolling green

hills of the Circle Ten Ranch stretched toward snowy mountain peaks far in the distance. Beside Jed, Mac Bullock, owner of both Miss Kitty Can Do and the Circle Ten Ranch, sighed mightily.

"You didn't drive such hard bargains a few years ago when all you could afford was an old gelding only worth five hundred dollars on a good day," Mac reminded him. "Now you're traipsin' around in five-hundred-dollars boots." But he grinned. "Howsome-ever, you got yourself a deal on Miss Kitty."

Jed grinned back, held out a hand, and they shook. "You sure have changed, boy," Mac commented for at least the tenth time. "Sure have."

"Reckon so."

Changed, yeah. He was working on himself, fixing himself up as if he'd never noticed what he looked like before, which he hadn't. As they walked silently past the huge barns and well-kept lawns that made up the nucleus of the Circle Ten, Jed took a moment to consider everything he'd bought since coming home from Sancia Island a month ago. He had a five-thousand-dollar gold watch and an expensive new wardrobe. He also had a black Ferrari and five new mares, some of which cost more than he'd made rodeoing in his entire life.

If money couldn't buy happiness, it could at least keep him distracted from thinking about Thena. Of course, among his purchases were two dozen books, whose titles included *Mystical Islands of the Georgia Coast*, *French for Beginners*, *Movie Classics of Yesteryear*, and *The Annotated Works of Charles Dickens*. He assured himself that just because he liked to spend all his spare time reading the subjects that interested her didn't mean that he thought about the lady herself all the time.

Mac's wife, Barbara, a stout brunette in dunga-rees and—as if it were usual ranch attire—a silk shirt, came out of the family's huge ranchhouse and crossed the yard excitedly, waving her arms. "Jed, if you don't find some way of letting that danged hotel of yours know how to reach you, your attorney's gonna have a conniption."

"It'd do him good," Jed drawled wryly. "He doesn't get much exercise."

"He's been lookin' for you for two days. The hotel manager traced you up here." Barbara held up a note she'd taken. "This is the message your lawyer left at the hotel: 'Trouble at your island,'" she read. "'Clients of mine were attacked by local woman and her dogs. Woman in jail. Dogs in jail. Clients pressing charges. Call me about this situation immediately.'"

Barbara Bullock looked up quizzically. "What kind of wild woman lives on your island?"

Jed was already running toward his truck. "One I hope to marry someday," he called back over his shoulder.

The Dundee municipal police force, which consisted of Chief Archie MacKay and Deputy Roy Payne, was casual and friendly. So was the municipal jail, which consisted of five cells with whitewashed concrete walls, a front desk, Archie's office, and a meeting room that doubled as Roy's office and the site of the local Masonic lodge.

Dundee had no dog pound, and Archie was too nice a man to send Rasputin and Godiva to the county pound, miles away, so he let them share Thena's cell. Her cell was cheerful by ordinary jail standards, but it was still a cell, with one high, narrow window in the back wall and a single, depressing light fixture overhead.

By standing on a chair, Thena could almost see out the window. As she had done every afternoon for the past three days, she perched on the cell's sturdy metal chair and tilted her face as close to the window as she could, worshiping the scent of fresh air and the narrow ray of sunlight. Rasputin and Godiva lay morosely on the cell bunk, their eyes trained on the window with a misery that equaled her own.

She might have to go to jail for weeks, even several months. The developers said she'd shot at them. In truth, she'd only fired the shotgun in the air, but it was four to one, their word against hers. The attorney appointed by the county had explained the possibility of a jail term. She couldn't afford the combination of her bail, a fine, and the hospital costs incurred by the two men Rasputin and Godiva had bitten.

Rasputin and Godiva . . . worst of all, the developers wanted them put to sleep, and the attorney had said that was a distinct possibility too. Her dear companions would die for crimes they had committed at her urging, minor crimes, just nibbles. They hadn't done much more than break the skin on two well-padded male rumps.

Thena wiped a few recalcitrant tears off her face and dried her hands on the gauzy yellow pants she wore with sandals and an orange top. She grasped the edge of the cell window with both hands and stood on tiptoe, straining to put her face directly in the midst of golden sunlight.

She heard the door to the cell area open, but didn't bother to turn around or get down from the chair. Roy, a round-faced young man with thinning black hair and wide eyes, wandered in periodically to offer sympathy and snacks, so Thena assumed that he had come to visit. She waited apathetically for his high-pitched voice to split the silence.

"Thena."

The voice was anything but high-pitched. Her name rumbled off it like low thunder. It was unmistakable.

Thena whirled around and got down from the chair with shaking legs. Her eyes flew to the calm, lean face and hazel eyes she'd drawn so lovingly, so many times. Jedidiah. Rasputin and Godiva clambered off the bunk, their tails wagging as if this traumatic situation finally made them admit that he was their friend.

But he wasn't a friend. He'd sent the developers. Thena didn't move, didn't speak as her long-simmering fury mingled with her shock. He looked back at her with troubled eyes, reading those emotions. Behind Jed, Roy stood grinning broadly.

"Mr. Powers has gotten all the charges dropped!" he chirped. "You're free! And the dogs too!" He stepped forward and unlocked the cell door.

Free. The word obliterated every other concern, including puzzlement over why Jed had come to help her. Thena cried out without meaning to and clasped her hands to her mouth. When the cell door opened, she rushed out with the dogs right behind her. Wordlessly, recklessly, she ran down the short hallway, flung open the door to the reception area, and headed for light and fresh air and freedom.

When Jed finally caught up with her, she was kneeling on the lawn in front of the jail, her face raised to the sun and the breeze. The dogs rolled in the grass with their own display of ecstasy.

Jed lowered himself beside her, sitting on his bootheels. She didn't acknowledge his presence at all, for which he was glad, because he needed a few seconds to swallow the lump in his throat. The sight of her wistfully trying to look out the window in the cell had torn him up. He understood her love for being outdoors; he knew what torture the cell must have been. He hurt for her. He cursed Chester Porter Thompson the fourth and his independent decision to send developers to Sancia.

"Miss Witch, you sure know how to get in trouble," he said softly.

She turned to look at him, her eyes glittering like cold silver stars. "I'll hate you for the rest of my life."

Nothing changed about Jed except the look on his

face, which went from tender to stunned. "I just got you off the hook," he reminded her in a distracted voice. Couldn't she see that he was innocent, that he was here because he loved her?

"But you let me sit in jail for three days, first. It was a terrific revenge tactic."

Stark, wounded anger replaced his amazement. "I didn't know what had happened until this mornin'. I caught the first plane out of Cheyenne, as soon as I heard."

She paused, surprised. Then a new thought flared inside her. "But you sent the developers." She wanted him to hurt the way she'd hurt during the past few days. "You're just a backwoods drifter with no concern for anyone or anything but yourself. How could I have ever thought you'd understand why Sancia is too beautiful to destroy? You don't know anything about beauty."

"My attorney sent the developers. I didn't even know they were comin' here, dammit."

"Your attorney is negotiating to sell Sancia?"

"Yep."

"At your direction."

He nodded slowly, defeated. "Yep."

She raked his new appearance with a disgusted gaze, arrogantly dismissing the creased slacks, the monogrammed sports shirt, the gleaming wristwatch, and the beautiful boots. "I don't know why I ever thought you were worth my trouble," she added, her voice breaking. "You can buy success, but you can't buy class. Your mother was a Gregg and she had class. But you didn't inherit it."

That was too much torment, too much provocation. He'd heard taunts like that before in his life, but none had ever hurt him more than these of Thena's. He struck back viciously. "Seein' as how you think so badly of me," Jed told her in a low, vibrating voice. "I'll live up to it. I'll bulldoze everything on Sancia and sell every horse for dog food. Includin' Cendrillon."

Neither of them was surprised when she slapped him. Jed stood slowly, barely noting the stinging of his jaw, feeling dead inside, his body following commands that he wasn't conscious of giving it. Thena stood too, staring up at him with a grief that momentarily eclipsed everything else. For one brief instant he thought she was going to reach out to him. But she turned quickly, called her dogs in a tearful voice, and walked toward the city docks, toward her island and her life. The man who loved her had just promised to destroy both.

Eight

Nothing could be more violent or more magnificent than the thunderstorms that crashed into the Georgia coasts every August. Ordinarily, Thena loved the wild lightning that streaked between the sky and the ocean; she loved to stand at the edge of the forest and let the wind tear at her hair and body. It made her feel closer to the world, and in the aftermath she was somehow new again.

But tonight's storm was an enemy that seemed to know that she was too depressed and tired to resist its battering force. Seeing Jed in Dundee that afternoon, hurting him and being hurt so badly in return, was all she could think about. The storm frightened the island horses, and Thena looked out her living room window to find the small herd gathered in the woods just beyond her yard. Cendrillon had led them to a spot she considered safer than any other.

The sight made Thena's chest tighten with love for them and fear for their future, both immediate and distant. Carrying a big lantern, she went outside in the cool, lashing rain and walked among the herd. Most of the horses knew her and let her touch their heads with a reassuring, gentle hand. The others, their eyes wide under soaked forelocks, retreated a little into the woods and watched her anxiously.

She stood for a long time, her head bowed, leaning against Cendrillon's warm shoulder.

Thena smelled the pungent warning in the air a few seconds before the lightning struck. She grasped Cendrillon's mane and screamed just as the bolt roared down from the night sky and split a huge live oak two dozen yards away. Thena stared in horror as the oak ripped from crown to roots. The torn halves fell in opposite directions, crushing the smaller trees and the palms.

Weak with fear, Thena woozily held the lantern up. She gasped and ran forward as the light revealed a gray yearling trapped under the limbs of the smoking, devastated tree. "Easy, *ma petite*," she soothed, stroking the colt's straining neck. He didn't seem to be hurt, just pinned. But his legs thrashed in wild resistance, and she knew it was simply a matter of time until he did hurt himself.

Thena studied the tree anxiously. The limbs were nearly a foot in diameter. She had nothing but an old, dull ax in the barn, so she couldn't cut them. Thena ran to get an old buggy collar and logging chains her grandfather had brought to the island. When she returned, she slid the collar over Cendrillon's steaming, wet neck and locked the heavy chains in place on either side.

It seemed to Thena that hours passed before she finally got the chains fastened around the tree. The gray colt lay still for periods, petrified by the strange activity, then thrashed dangerously until he was too tired to continue.

Nearly exhausted herself, breathing raggedly, water streaming down her face, Thena went to Cendrillon's head and wound a hand in the little mare's mane. "Pull, *chérie*, pull!" Cendrillon's small hooves dug into the thick, sandy soil. Her neck bowed down and her haunches flexed with tremendous effort. The tree limbs slid nearly a foot, skimming lightly from the colt's barrel to his hindquarters. He squealed in new terror and began to fight, hanging a hind foot in the smaller limbs.

"Quiet, stay quiet!" Thena called to him. She unbuckled the chains so that Cendrillon was free, then ran to the colt's side and knelt down, trying to ease his leg out of the tangled branches. "We're going to get you out of this, somehow! There's got to be a way—"

A tremendous clap of thunder nearly deafened her. The colt lurched up on his front legs and fell back. Thena wrapped both arms around his neck and tried to hold him down. The wind gusted sharply, and Thena cringed as a two-hundred-foot pine tree toppled beyond the far side of the barn.

It was difficult to think rationally amidst such awesome violence. Suddenly Thena cried out at the thought of what Sarah Gregg must have gone through, the overwhelming fear and desperation as she fought to save her Arabians from the hurricane almost forty-five years ago. H. Wilkens had found her pinned under a tree much like this one, her neck broken. Thena's heart pounded with dread while she looked at deep, dancing shadows as the oaks flung themselves back and forth in the lantern light. "Sarah!" she screamed as if begging for help. "Sarah!"

The wind howled. Thena pressed her face into the colt's soggy gray mane and cupped her hands over his eyes to shield them from the rain a little. The dogs crept up and huddled by her again; Cendrillon stood in the edge of the lantern light, snorting and jumping every time a limb cracked somewhere in the woods.

A few minutes later, Thena heard a repetitive splashing sound through the din. She squinted into the darkness with alarm, watching Cendrillon twist about and stare toward the sound too. The dogs barked lustily, but without malice. Thena turned to look at them in bewilderment, amazed at the welcoming tone of their voices. When she looked back her breath caught in her throat.

A figure in a yellow, hooded rain slicker appeared in the lantern light. Even before the hood fell back, Thena recognized Jed's tense face in the shadows. A deep, serene conviction flowed through her, even though she knew it was highly imaginative. But why else would he be here at night, in a storm? Sarah had drawn her grandson home.

"Jedidiah!" He knelt in the rain beside her, his eyes frozen on her face. He grabbed her shoulders with rough hands.

"Are you hurt?" Jed yelled.

She shook her head. "But Cendrillon can't pull this limb off the colt! She needs help!"

His hands left her shoulders, cupped her face, smoothed her matted hair back, and traced the contours of her wet skin as if he were convincing himself that she was truly all right. He pulled the rain slicker off and draped it around her shoulders, then he walked quickly to Cendrillon. Thena stroked the colt's head as Jed turned the mare around and reattached the chains.

This time, as the mare pulled, Jed pulled too. Thena scrambled up and tugged the branches away from the colt's hind leg. The big limbs over his body moved by inches, but they moved. And five minutes later, the colt leapt to his feet, free. He galloped vigorously into the woods.

Thena staggered to Cendrillon, feeling giddy, and helped Jed remove the logging chains and collar. Then she slapped the shaking mare on the shoulder and yelled, "Follow your friend and keep him out of trouble!" Cendrillon disappeared into the inky forest at a trot, her white tail streaming out behind her with ghostly luminescence.

Thena faced Jed, her chest heaving, and the shock of his sudden appearance began to register. His rich brown hair was plastered to his head and he was breathing just as hard as she was. They stared at each other for several seconds, no words capable of asking or answering all the questions that hung in the air. Finally he bent and got the lantern. By some silent signal, they walked to the porch, where the dogs had already retreated now that the excitement was over.

Or was it over? The storm around them was beginning to fade, but there were other tempests to consider. Thena sat down on the top of the porch steps. Jed sat down beside her, and she gazed in amazement at the dirty mess that had once been his very nice pair of western boots. His soaked slacks and sports shirt clung to the athletic contours of his body.

He ran his hands across his hair and frowned at her frank scrutiny of his ruined appearance. "No class," he said tersely. "Just like you told me."

Thena faced forward and lowered her head into her hands. "What kind of crazy man did you hire to bring you to Sancia at night, in a storm?"

"Farlo. Who else? But the storm hadn't started when we left Dundee. Once he left me at your dock, it took almost an hour to walk here."

"Thank you for what you did just now." Thena fumbled to make sense out of all that had happened. "You helped save a horse you plan to turn into dog food."

"Oh, hell." The exasperation in his voice hinted that she knew better than to believe what he'd said earlier about the horses.

Thena held out her hands and looked at him in angry supplication. "Then why are you here? What do you want now?"

His mouth thinned in dismay. "It's my island, and I reckon I can visit it anytime I want to."

"In the dark, in a storm?"

Her haggling destroyed his patience and accomplished the nearly impossible. It made him yell. "Yes, dammit, in the dark and in a storm!" He reached into a back pocket on his slacks and withdrew a document, which he presented to her stiffly. "The deed," he rasped. "Take it. This heap of shells and everything on it isn't mine anymore. It's yours."

Thena stared at him in speechless shock. Her face pale, her stomach tingling with a disturbing hint that she might cry, Thena took the paper and glanced at it. True. Unbelievable, but true. Sancia was hers.

Her voice sounded small and fractured. "Why, Jedidiah?" She couldn't look at him. She couldn't think.

"I want you to understand something," he answered fiercely. Her gaze came up and absorbed the pride and dignity in his expression. "I do have class. I can recognize somethin' beautiful when I see it. I've seen it in Wyoming, out there in mountains that make a man want to cry because they're so pretty, and in prairies that go on forever until you think that the sky is the only thing that brings 'em to an end. And I've seen what's beautiful here. I don't understand this kind of beauty, but I know it's special. I think you know that I couldn't ever have gone through with those godawful things I said today. I can't hurt this place . . . and I can't . . . hurt you."

He stood and went down the porch steps, then turned to glare up at her. The rain had become a slow drizzle that misted his face and hair. "I'm a damn fool, and you can enjoy that fact after I leave. I've got some camping gear on the dock. I'll stay there tonight and Farlo'll be back for me in the mornin'." When she started to speak, he held up a warning hand. "If you've got thanks, hold 'em. I didn't expect 'em when I decided to give you the island. It's always belonged to you. I just made it official." He paused, looking even more upset. "And if you've got more ugly names to call me, hold those too. I've had enough to last me a long time."

Thena pounded her knees with both fists. "You

pick the worst time to become a talkative man!" She stood and hurried down the steps, and before he knew what was happening, she wrapped her arms around his neck and hugged him, hugged him as if she'd never let him go. Jed's hand rose uncertainly to touch her shoulders.

"You don't have to do anything in return," he groaned, trying to push her away. "Don't latch on to me out of gratitude."

"You stubborn cowboy, I'm latching on to you because I've missed you and because I love you!" Thena tilted her head back and looked at him through a haze of bittersweet anxiety. "I wanted you to come back. I prayed that you'd come back. And it had nothing to do with the island." She shook his shoulders. "It had to do with me, Jedidiah. You and I are two of a kind."

His arms moved slowly around her back, while he absorbed the soft, silver light in her eyes. "You love me?" he asked numbly.

Unable to tell whether he found that good or bad at this point, she tried to sound practical about it. "The immediate chemical reaction can be explained as a routine, though perhaps unusually fervent, mating desire, but the spiritual bond that grew between us is something unique." She hesitated as she saw the gleaming intensity rising in his eyes, not quite sure what he meant to do about her revelation. "Do you think you want that kind of bond, Jedidiah? The powerful, permanent kind?"

Jed's next words, simple and heartfelt, left her gazing at him in adoring wonder. "I think," he murmured, "that it's my destiny to walk where you walk and love what you love for the rest of my life."

Dizzy with emotion, Thena closed her eyes. She had both Sancia and Jed. It was incredible. Jed touched his mouth to hers, and she stiffened with fear. Of course it was incredible, Thena thought suddenly. And impossible. She knew how to love, but she didn't know how to make love, and nothing could overcome that inadequacy. Thena arched her head back, away from his kiss, and looked up to find his face gone ashen.

"What am I doin' wrong this time?" he asked gruffly. "Just tell me. I never had this trouble before, and I'll be damned if I'm gonna ruin what you feel for me."

Thena's heart nearly burst with devotion. There wasn't another man in the world who would assume that her awkwardness was due to some mistake on his part. "Let's get out of the rain, Jedidiah." She pushed herself from his embrace and went back to the porch, feeling flushed and anxious. He followed quickly, his face set in a worried frown.

"You can stay in the upstairs bedroom," she said with as much lightness as she could manage. Thena opened the screen door and stepped inside. He came after her, his concerned gaze scouring her face. "Come along. I'll give you those baggy old clothes you found so funny before. After we're both dry, I'll fix some hot tea—"

"Are you too much of a coward to just tell me the truth?" His voice was low and firm. "We just said we love each other. Now you're actin' strange again. You owe me the truth."

Thena laughed shakily as she turned to face him. "That I secretly like the way you look in my father's old clothes? All right, I admit it. The way the calves of your hairy legs show under the rolled-up pants—"

"Thena, for God's sake, if you don't want to be physical with me, just tell me why and be done with it."

She backed away, shaking her head. "Do we have to talk about that right now? What about romance? Friendship—"

"What about fear," he interjected. "You're plain scared of me, and it hurts me right down where I live. I want to make love to you, every time you touch me I imagine how it'd be, every time you look at me, every time I get near you and catch the scent of your hair and skin. . . . I think about you at night. I dream about holding you and wake up so ready it makes me want to burst."

"Oh, Jedidiah, don't," she whispered. "I don't deserve that kind of desire." But the floods of sensation provoked by his words told her that she desperately wanted him to desire her that way, and she wished with every part of her soul that she knew how to make his dreams come true.

He continued doggedly. "Thena, the best love in the world is the one that mixes romance and friendship with bedroom pleasures. That's what we could have. Don't you want that?"

"Certainly." She went to the kitchen area, took a dishcloth in her trembling hands, and pretended to be thoroughly involved in drying her hair. "I'm in shock, Jedidiah. You just gave me an island, for goodness' sake. I'm overwhelmed. I can't think about you and Sancia all at once."

Her heart skipped beats as she heard Jed's heavy boots crossing the floor. He stopped behind her, and she could feel his bewilderment and frustration. "The professor, Nate Gallagher," he began in a carefully neutral voice. "I reckon nothing could replace what you had with him. Is that it? You can't touch me without thinkin' about him."

"No, that's not it. I cared about Nate very much. I worshiped him for his wisdom, his grasp of philosophy, his curiosity and creativity. But it wasn't like . . . it wasn't the same as the feelings between us." Nate didn't want me, she added silently. I couldn't make him want me, ever. And I never wanted him the way I want you.

"That doesn't explain a whole lot to me, except I'm wonderin' if there was somebody else other than Nate."

"No." She turned around, fumbling with the towel, too close to revealing everything about her shame.

Thena stared at the floor. "No one else. I met Nate when I was eighteen. So there's just been Nate." Her eyes, very guarded, rose slowly to meet Jed's. "And you."

He tried not to show how surprised he was. Now he could figure out some of her mystery. Innocence. Not just innocence about how the rest of the world lived, but innocent about men. If he'd felt protective for her in the past, now he felt like Sir Galahad. Jed tilted his head to one side and made sure his voice was utterly gentle. "Did he hurt you some way? In bed, I mean? Are you afraid it'll be like that with me?"

She shook her head, her expression nearly crumbling, and whispered, "No."

He took a step toward her and she frantically grasped the edge of the sink behind her, feeling trapped. Jed halted. She looked as if she'd do anything to stay away from him. He closed the distance between them in two strides and caught her shoulders in a firm grip. Her eyes filled with despair.

"What are you afraid of?" he demanded.

"Nothing."

"God woman! Tell me! Just tell me!"

"Do we have to have sex? Is it so crucial—"

"It's damn crucial that you tell me what's wrong so we can talk about how to deal with it!"

"I'm afraid I'd disappoint you! I don't know how to make love!" She blurted the words out and buried her face in her hands.

"What the hell—"

"I don't know how," she repeated tearfully. "You've been disappointed in me already. In the way I kiss—or rather, don't kiss."

She raised her head and went on blindly, staring into his incredulous expression. "Don't you see? Some people are just not suited to be sexual. They're thinkers, not . . . doers."

After a long minute, he asked blankly, "Weren't you a 'doer' with Nate?"

"Not . . . exactly. I learned from him that some women like . . . well, like Sophia Loren . . . have talents that are physical. Other women, such as me, have talents that are intellectual. I don't excite men. Except for you, but you're special." Thena looked at him with misery in her eyes. "I don't have any of the natural talent that I'm sure you expect in a woman. I don't think going to bed with me would make you happy."

He let go of her, turned, and walked away, his hands on his hips and his head down in thought. "Answer one question straight for me," he said slowly, "so I'll know I'm understandin' this craziness right. Did you and the professor ever make love?"

"No."

"Have you ever made love to anyone?"

Thena's heart sank. She didn't have any defenses left. "No. I'm a twenty-five-year-old . . . old maid."

He pondered everything she'd told him. Finally, his back still to her, he said, "Go put on some dry clothes. I've got to think on this awhile longer."

Thena suppressed a sob. He was uncertain and disappointed, just as she'd thought. "Of course," she murmured. She hurried past him, went into her bedroom, and shut the door.

She dreaded going back into the main part of the house, so she took her time. She heard Jed go upstairs and come back down a few minutes later. She heard him moving around the kitchen, and eventually she heard her teapot whistle. Morose, Thena slipped into a soft, light blue cotton smock. It was one of her most comfortable dresses and she needed the security it offered her. With its colorful embroidery, it always made her feel like the queen of the forest. Tonight, it didn't help her mood much, and the soft fabric somehow felt scratchy on her breasts, which were strangely sensitive and hot.

Barefoot, her hair loosely braided down her back, Thena walked out of her room and stopped, amazed. The living room was shadowy, lit only by a reading lamp beside one end of the couch and a small fixture over the kitchen sink. Jed stood at the sink, fixing the tea. He was barefoot, too, and he wore only the white pants with the legs rolled up.

Thena's heart rate leapt at the sight of his bare, strong back, sculpted by years of hard work, his corded arms with their dark hair, the straight, smooth length of his waist, and the powerful way it curved into his tight flanks and rump. What was going on here? A seduction? Hadn't he heard anything she'd said about herself?

Nine

He turned gracefully, studied her for a moment, then nodded toward the couch. "Sit yourself down, Miss Witch."

She did, her legs barely working, her hands lightly clenched. He walked across the room carrying two mugs of steaming tea, and the shadows seemed to emphasize every masculine angle and plane in his body. He sat down in one corner of the couch—the dark corner, Thena noted breathlessly—and motioned with a slight movement of his head.

"Come over here," he said gently. "I'm gonna put my arm around your shoulders."

Thena's pulse beat faster. Even though his voice was familiar, his eyes seemed lit by an alien fire. But at least she could tell, now, that he wasn't uncomfortable because of what she'd said earlier, and that was all that mattered. Thena moved within the arch of the arm he stretched out, then took her cup of tea from him and stared down into it as his arm curled tenderly around her shoulders. The coarseness of his fingers, which drew small circles on her bare arm, sent pleasant quivers through her. Thena tilted her head to study his hands. She knew every ridge and scar of them. She'd lovingly committed them to memory.

He seemed inclinced not to talk, and after a minute she settled into the same mood. She took a swallow of tea, glanced at him, then looked away. "I'm sorry for what I said today," she murmured. "I blamed you for everything. I was wrong. The things I called you—"

"Were just a mistake. Forget it."

"Jedidiah, I didn't mean them."

He exhaled wearily. "Gal, I have to be honest with you." He pulled her closer to him and talked slowly, softly, for a long time. He explained how awkward he felt in his new role as a millionaire. He wasn't accustomed to traveling on airplanes or staying in big hotels or eating in fine restaurants. He'd never feel comfortable in the social circles to which his money admitted him, and he worried about managing that money even though he had an attorney, an accountant, and a stockbroker to help him.

Thena sensed that it was difficult for him to admit his worries and inadequacies in those matters, and her chest swelled with a tender sense of pride and protectiveness. He was so strong in so many ways that this vulnerable side of him only made him more human, more lovable. She relaxed into the crook of his arm and drew her feet under her so she could snuggle closer to him. She knew this careful, unhurried mood of his was calculated to loosen her tight nerves, and she didn't resist the effort.

"Nate," he said kindly. "I want to know about this Nate hombre."

Tension wound around her again. After a long pause, she cleared her throat and said, "You have to understand why I feel so awkward about touching you or kissing you. I tried those things with Nate, and they never worked the way my books said they're supposed to."

"Sometimes I think you read too much, gal. You can't learn everything from books. Or from old movies."

Thena took a sip of tea, but couldn't really taste it. She was too distracted by Jed's words and the whirl of sensation that came from him—his damp, fresh scent, the heat of his fingers, the warmth of his body, the scorching intensity of his eyes. She struggled for more explanations about Nate.

"He drank a lot," she finally managed. "He was fifteen years older than me. He'd been married once, a long time ago."

"How much did he drink?"

She sighed. "He was unquestionably a severe alcoholic. But he was a brilliant man, a very controlled man, and he never let the drinking show. Only a few people knew."

"And this dude told you that you weren't sexy?"

She nodded. "He wasn't mean about it. He was very logical. And I proved him right." She looked up with a determined glint in her eyes. "I humiliated myself many times, trying to get him to . . . make love to me. I always failed. No other woman would have."

"No other man could have resisted you."

Thena looked at him in askance. "If you're saying that he wasn't normal, you're wrong. Nate looked like Richard Burton, and he had incredible charisma. He was always flirting with women on the mainland. They chased him like crazy."

"That doesn't mean he was A-okay. Did he ever let any of them catch him?"

"No, he wasn't interested in what he called 'sexual dalliances.' He was perfectly loyal to me."

"So what'd he do about it?"

"He wrote poetry about me. He held my hand." Her eyes flickered with painful memories. "He'd fall asleep on the beach sometimes when we were reading together. I . . . uhmmm, would lie down beside him, and sometimes he'd put one arm over me. He'd hug me and hold me. Sometimes he'd give me a kiss on the forehead." She took a deep sip of tea. "It's embarrassing to talk about this to you, Jedidiah."

"Don't feel that way. I want you to talk about what

went on between you and Nate. I'm beginnin' to think that I understand him better than you do." He took her cup and set it on the floor with his. Then he grasped her hand and held it firmly. His eyes weren't alien any longer. They were full of compassion.

"Nate would have made love to you," Jed arched one brow in silent innuendo, "if he could have."

"Oh, you don't mean—"

"Heavy drinkers can't, a lot of times. My pa couldn't, the last few years. The doc said it was the booze. Give up booze or do without girls, he told him. Pa said girls weren't much fun without booze, so he kept drinkin'."

"Are you insinuating that Nate was simply protecting his masculine pride?"

"Yep. Trust me on this one, gal. I know human nature better than you do. Especially a man's."

She blinked rapidly, thinking. Then she shook her head. "It's possible, but . . ."

"It's probable, gal." He tilted her chin up and held her gaze with his dark, reassuring eyes. "Nate buffaloed you. There's not anything wrong with you that practice won't fix."

"I can't even kiss correctly," she reminded him. Her breathing was so shallow that she was almost faint. "Are you saying that you don't mind playing teacher? That you're not horribly disappointed and shocked? Do you know any other twenty-five-year-old maiden women?"

Loving her made Jed feel that he was a new man, capable of amazing new accomplishments. He'd never considered himself an expert on romance before, but he reveled in the idea. For the first time in his life, he was concerned only with giving, not taking, happiness.

"Pretty lady, I'll love teachin' you," he whispered. Humor glinted in his eyes. "I'm not disappointed to find out you're an old maid. I'm just sorry you didn't explain all this to me a month ago."

"I was ashamed."

"Nothing to be ashamed of. You're not old, and"—he dropped the humor and became serious—"before the night's over, I suspect you won't be a 'maid.' " His undemanding tone of voice told her that he was patient. "If you'd like to try makin' love with me, that is."

"Yes. I'll certainly try." Her eyes were bright with tears and her tone was full of solemn determination, as if he'd just asked her to recite every category in the Dewey decimal system. Jed smiled sympathetically. He'd have to overwhelm her serious attitude.

"Then everything will be just fine." He brushed his lips across her face, starting at her hairline and working down to her mouth.

"If I'm a terrible student, what then?" The anxiety in her voice made him hug her tightly. "Will it ruin everything? Will you be honest and tell me that Nate's assessment of my abilities was accurate?"

He nuzzled her cheek. Tentatively, she nuzzled back." Wildflower, you got it all wrong," he murmured against her ear. "There's no way you could get an F in my class, 'cause there aren't any grades. There aren't any rules. You do what gives you pleasure, and it'll just naturally please me too."

"That sounds too simple," she protested raggedly.

"Try it. You kiss me. Kiss me whatever way you want to. Just use your imagination." She looked at him uncertainly, her face flushed and her lips parted. His eyes challenged her with gentle devilry. "Do it," he dared. "You want to do it. You know you want to."

"You're a tease," she protested, leaning toward him a little.

His voice dropped to a throaty rumble. "I love you. I see that sweetness behind your eyes and I know you love me too. We haven't been together a long time, but that doesn't matter, 'cause we're two of a kind, like you said before. Hardheaded loners with a lot of bad memories and a big, hurtin' need to find one special person to care about. With all that goin' for us, this sex stuff you're worried about isn't even important."

Thena uttered a happy sound and pressed her lips to one corner of his mouth. She hovered over the spot, looking at his mouth with half-shut eyes. "I should just do what I want to you, Jedidiah?"

"Yep. But you gotta kiss the other corner too," he noted coyly. "Otherwise I'll be lopsided." She kissed it. "Ain't no limit on the number of kisses I'm willin' to accept," he murmured. "Help yourself."

He settled deeper into the couch and stroked her back languidly as Thena placed small, light kisses all over his face. Her breath quickened; the kisses quickened, and suddenly her hands slid up his chest. "Not bad," he assured her in a voice that strained for nonchalance.

"Where do you like to be touched?" she asked hoarsely.

He pointed to the slight indention at the center of his chest. She ran her fingers through the curly hair and explored the skin underneath. "And here." Jed pointed to the base of his throat. "I reckon"—he barely repressed a smile—"that a kiss on the spot would feel awful good too."

She bent her head and put her lips in the small valley between his collarbones. Thena felt his pulse racing against her mouth and loved the hot and musky scent of his skin. She couldn't resist the urge to touch her tongue to it, tasting the masculine flavor. He groaned and she lifted her head quickly, frowning.

"Did I do something wrong?"

"Yep. You stopped too soon." He grinned at her, and she noticed for the first time that his face was as flushed as hers. "Thena, my sweet darlin', there isn't a wrong way or a right way to do these things. Look, you don't have any notion to bite me or somethin' painful like that, do you?" She shook her head. "Then quit worryin' and do what you want." He let his head fall back on the couch dramatically. "I'll just have to make myself enjoy it."

His teasing and reassurance provoked her beyond caring whether she made mistakes or not. Thena took his face between her hands and covered his mouth with an unrestrained, intimate kiss. When his lips parted, she met his rough, delicious tongue with her own. And quite naturally, as if she'd known what to do all along, she gave and accepted a sensuous exploration. Suddenly she pulled away, laughing dizzily. Thena threw her arms around his neck and hugged him.

"It's wonderful! Just wonderful! I had no idea!"

He chuckled in delight. "You ain't seen nothin' yet."

"Wait! I have to do it again!" This time the kiss went on for nearly a minute. And suddenly it wasn't a game any longer. The mood turned serious as Jed's long arms snaked around her waist and he taught her kissing maneuvers she'd never read about in books. There was something possessive and demanding about him now, a dark, mysterious need that could have been frightening, but wasn't. Thena not only understood the need, she ached with it herself.

She wasn't certain when she shifted position, but suddenly she realized that she was sitting on his lap. Her lips weren't frozen with nervousness anymore, they were mobile and capricious, capturing his mouth repeatedly and being captured in return.

"So where do you like to be kissed?" he asked playfully, as his mouth trailed down the side of her neck.

"I don't know, I never thought about it . . . but . . . there! And . . . that's nice . . . very nice . . . oh, that spot too . . . Jedidiah, is it supposed to feel so fantastic everywhere?"

"You ain't seen nothin' yet," he repeated.

She held tightly to him and her head fell back as he proved that every inch of her neck and shoulders was capable of responding with the same tingling pleasure. His mouth burned the skin just above her smock's bodice, and the heat radiated down her breasts and stomach. Thena raised her head and looked at Jed solemnly.

"I think we should lie down on the couch," she whispered. "That would seem to me more comfortable."

"Oh, yes, ma'am. Lots more."

Thena had never expected the simple act of changing places to be so thrilling. She stretched out on her back, every nerve singing with anticipation. It felt so right to lie there unguarded, looking up at Jed with trusting eyes. He lowered his body next to hers, sliding one hand over her stomach and the other under her head. His gaze was serious as he nestled the length of her torso against his own.

Her thigh settled against the lower part of his body and encountered an unmistakable and dramatic ridge. Thena's eyes went quickly to Jed's, and her amazed, thoughtful expression made him smile. Her insides, which had already turned to a jumble of sensations as his hand stroked her stomach, now melted entirely.

She felt infused with a heat of rising intensity and a tender desire to give him as much pleasure as he gave her. "My books didn't explain this very well," she whispered. "They never talked about the feeling of harmony." She reached out cautiously and began to stroke the powerful, sheathed muscles of his bare stomach. Her fingers moved over the front of his pants and very very carefully touched the stiffness pressing against her leg. "We haven't even made love yet," she continued in an awed voice, "but I already feel as if you've become a part of me."

"We don't have to join our bodies to be makin' love," he told her softly. "Touchin' each other, talkin' to each other, puttin' good feelings behind everything we do for each other—that's what makes this different from what you've read in your sex books." And from anything I've ever shared with a woman before, he added silently.

He nestled his head next to hers, and Thena turned her face so that they could kiss easily. The fresh-washed night air was fragrant, and the only sound was the low hum of crickets outside. There seemed to be no world beyond their peaceful spot, nothing except the two of them in the shadowy light, their hands moving languidly over each other's body.

Thena gave up her memories, her fears. Jed's touch brought her to a heightened level of awareness where only the present mattered. She felt more alive and vibrant than ever before. When he slid her bodice down and cupped each of her breasts in his palms, she thought nothing could surpass the intense pleasure. But that was just the beginning.

His lips on her nipples proved almost too exquisite to bear in silence. His hands, easing her dress down her thighs, were inclined to wander in a way that made her body rise to welcome them. He touched her intimately, and she responded with a natural zeal that amazed her. She didn't know herself anymore. She only knew that her life was beginning a second time, tonight.

He was a very quiet man under any circumstances, but even more so now. By the time he cradled her naked body in his arms, shivering with emotion, the fire within him seemed to have robbed him of all speech. He just looked at her with eyes that gleamed with hunger and devotion.

"My bedroom," she said simply. And he nodded.

He carried her there in the dark and laid her down on the center of the white coverlet. Thena put her hands on the pillow behind her head and watched him move around the bed, loosening the white netting from its ties on the bedposts. The gossamer folds cascaded around her so that she seemed to be floating in a cloud.

Thena kept her eyes locked on Jed greedily, but he moved at an unhurried, provocative pace that built the tension to a hypnotizing level. He lit a small kerosene lamp on the dresser by the window, then walked to the side of the bed and stood quietly, facing her. He slid the white pants down his lean hips and stepped out of them without ever taking his gaze from hers.

The slight catching of her breath conveyed her appreciation of all he revealed. She moved over and placed her hand on the spot next to her. Jed parted the filmy netting, knelt on the bed, and held out his hands as if asking for an invitation. Her eyes glowing like silver jewels, she grasped them and drew him to her.

Jed gathered her in his arms. "I won't hurt you," he promised in a throaty whisper.

And he didn't. The entry of his body into hers was a moment of ecstasy that made them both lie very still for a second, smiling at each other and whispering soft, loving words. Then he began a deep, easy rhythm that quickly captured them in an ancient and mindless cadence of pleasure.

A slight breeze curled into the room and carried their moans away on its currents. Thena loved the way the granitelike length of him fit snugly inside her, as if she had never been complete until she joined with him. His movements were strong and yet careful. They created a whirlwind of sensation and blinding emotion in her, consuming rational thought, bonding her soul to his.

Thena raised herself to him, held him with a wantonness that brought hoarse cries of happiness from his throat and provoked him to lose his tenuous control. For a single, beautifully paralyzing moment they reached beyond the edge of mortality together and created a pure dream that would never die.

Thena weakly sank her fingers into his damp hair and closed her eyes in slow, helpless wonder as the aftermath of intense sensation pulsated through her. More than a minute passed before she became aware of Jed's dazed voice, thick and husky, whispering against her mouth. Apparently he'd been speaking to her for some time.

"Answer me, Thena. Dear God, answer me, sweetheart. Are you all right?"

For once, she was the one without words. She looked at him and nodded blankly, then feathered her lips across his face, kissing the concern out of every feature with a care that bordered on reverence. She gave him a distracted smile, and his face tightened with new worry.

"I've never seen you like this," he persisted.

When she finally spoke, her voice was the essence of contentment. "That's because you've never seen me this happy before, Jedidiah." Thena paused, her glowing eyes riveted to his. "I've never been so happy in my entire life."

Relief burst out of him in a long, low sigh. "Was makin' love all you hoped it would be?" His hands stroked her tangled hair, undoing the shambles that remained of her braid.

There was no hesitation to her answer. It was a blissful smile and a soft, "Yes. Oh, yes."

"You belong to me, Thena. And I belong to you. I reckon that kind of talk sounds awful possessive, but . . ."

She pulled him to her for a long, deep kiss. Then she said, in a voice that made his heart swell with every breath he took, "I've belonged to you since the day we met. I've belonged to you all my life, Jedidiah."

And then he knew, deep down where his bad feelings for his grandfather Gregg wouldn't let him admit it yet, that he'd been waiting for years to come to her and this island, and that he was finally home.

• • •

"Jedidiah's very handsome, isn't he, *ma petites*? His nose is a little crooked and he has tiny scars everywhere—well, almost everywhere—but that only adds to the appeal, doesn't it? It makes me want to be gentle with him. He had a hard life growing up on the mainland, you see."

Coming lazily out of sleep, Jed heard those tender words. Smiling, he opened his eyes to the filtered light of mid-morning and inhaled deeply. This place had the freshest, best air on earth, he thought. This was the third day he'd wakened in Thena's glorious old bed, and waking up got better every time.

He raised his head a bit and eyed Thena sitting on a colorful old rug by the windowsill. Naked, her dark hair brushing halfway down her back, her legs folded under her and her hands resting quietly in her lap, she looked like a beautiful reincarnation of Tasoneela paying an Indian tribute to a tribe of wrens. He grinned. She talked to spirits and birds and God alone knew what else. And they probably answered in some way he hadn't figured out yet.

She had her head turned so that she didn't see Jed watching her raptly, and she continued chatting to the dozen tiny birds that pecked and chirped over the seed she'd spread on the sill.

"Did you know," she asked them with a happy sigh, "that there are wrens just like you in Wyoming? Jedidiah said so. How do you think I'd like it out there? Maybe I'll visit, someday." Her voice had been low to begin with. Now it dropped, and he had to strain to hear it. "But we'll just have to convince him to live here on Sancia, won't we? He can't live out West. He belongs here. This is a large island. There'd be plenty of room for a herd of quarter horses."

Jed's head sank back on the pillow. Oh, no, Miss Witch, he promised silently. This place might be more likable than he had thought at first, but it would never claim him. He'd stay and enjoy it for a few weeks, then coax her out West. She owned Sancia now, and no one would harm it or its damned old Gregg mansion when she went away. It would always be here for her to visit, and he'd make sure she got to visit as often as she wanted.

Jed shut his eyes and pretended to be asleep when he heard her bare feet tiptoeing across the creaky floor toward him. She was still a little cautious of him because of her inexperience, and he didn't want her to be unnerved by the unusually intense morning arousal that was throbbing underneath her white coverlet.

Last night he'd awakened to find her propped on one elbow close beside him, her fingertips feathering timidly over the hair on his chest. When she'd realized that she'd disturbed his sleep, she was embarrassed. He heartily and rather abruptly showed her just how happy he was to be disturbed, and when he finished, she was silent and quivering slightly. He'd wanted to ask if he'd scared her, but hadn't because he dreaded that she'd confirm it.

The covers rustled and the mattress sank beside him as she slipped back into bed. Stay calm, Jed urged himself. Don't breath faster, dammit. No, your hands aren't gonna just casually inch toward her. Be still. That's it, pardner, breath slow, keep your hands still, let her go back to sleep. . . .

"Hmmm," she sighed. Her warm, pliant body nestled close to him by tantalizing degrees, breasts indenting against his forearm, loins cushioning his hip, hand sliding softly across his chest and down the center of his stomach. Jed couldn't help the way his back arched in response. When her fingers found what he'd tried to ignore, they rushed over it in tender amazement. "Oh, my," she whispered, sounding stunned.

His ruse was hopelessly destroyed. "I'm tryin' to show you that I'm not always a wild-eyed goat," he protested, as his eyes flickered open in dismay. "I was pretty charged up last night and I don't want you to think . . . I was tryin' to let you go back to sleep without bein' attacked right now." Jed turned his head against the downy pillow and gazed at her with apology. "It's okay, gal. That part of me's got a mind of its own in the mornin'. You don't have to feel obligated. . . ."

"I got a hankerin' for you, boy," she whispered in a perfect imitation of his drawl. "Don't go lily-livered on me. I reckon I know what I want, and I ain't scared of gettin' it."

With her funny accent she sounded like a Cajun Scarlett O'Hara, and when she mixed it with a cowboy drawl the result was hysterical. Jed laughed until he could barely breathe.

"I can see I worried for nothin'," he finally rasped. "You're gettin' too big for your britches, gal."

"I got no britches," she drawled solemnly.

"Let me check. Yep. No britches."

"I got no patience." Her hands moved over him wantonly. "I got no shyness. This filly has turned wild."

They wrestled playfully, and she won by straddling his thighs and holding his head by both ears. Jed wound a hand in her long hair and pulled her down for a deep, satisfying kiss. "Reckon you need some tamin'," he murmured. "Reckon I'll stay on this pile of sand awhile and see if I can make you behave."

She radiated happiness as she looked down at him. "I love you, cowboy."

"I love you."

He held her so tightly that he felt her heart beating against his ribs. Or maybe they shared the same heart. It seemed possible. Anything seemed possible here, with her. Anything, that is, except her plan for him to stay.

Ten

Days turned into weeks. Weeks turned into a month, and September's cooler breezes made the island temperatures drop to idyllic levels. Jed never brought up the subject of the two of them leaving the island. He started to at times, but a strange, troubled intuition always stopped him. He knew that part of it was sheer contentment.

He couldn't deny that he loved the lazy, timeless passing of days marked only by sunrises, sunsets, and the rhythm of the tides. He'd head back to reality before long, but in the meantime he'd spend his hours making love to Thena, watching her paint, and helping her catalog the minute, whimsical details of flora and fauna and weather. She was his whole life.

At night he read her books. At first he felt self-conscious, as if a grown man ought to be embarrassed for liking make-believe stories. But with Thena's encouragement, the books became something he treasured. He and she would read for hours in bed, and then one or the other would reach out an inviting hand, and the reading would be over for another night.

Beneba Everett radioed one windy afternoon that she was coming to dinner, and they took Thena's rattling, lurching truck to the dock to meet her. Jed politely held his laughter as her small motorboat bounced toward them. Buffeted by the wind, it looked like a drunken water beetle.

When the beetle finally bobbed next to the dock, Beneba refused Jed's helping hand and clambered out with a spryness that amazed him. The elderly black munchkin hugged Thena and after Thena's introduction, grunted a hello to him in her low Gullah accent. Then she plopped a basket full of string beans and her personal belongings into his arms.

As she paraded to the truck, Jed stared after her. Beneba was comical but innately dignified, with eyes that held an ethereal light. Old gal probably had cataracts, Jed decided, and that accounted for the eerie blue-white cast to those dark peepers. Her bare feet churned the sand with youthful vigor, and her kinky gray hair bounced in a long braid. Her coffee-colored skin was wrinkled, her arms and legs lithe, and her oversized print dress had a wild gardenia pinned to one shoulder.

She was sort of a wild gardenia herself, he decided. And she had the commanding manner of an ancient sage. "Yoda," Jed whispered to Thena out of the corner of his mouth.

"What is a 'Yoda'?" she whispered back.

"Aw, I've gotta get you some current movies, gal." Grinning, he hoisted the basket to his shoulder.

After they reached the house, Beneba puckered the entirety of her dark face around a clay pipe and spent every spare minute squinting at Jed in an assessing way. He secretly renamed her Popeye and squinted back.

The three of them sat on the porch shelling beans, and even he, with his taciturn nature, was surprised by the lack of conversation. Beneba seemed perfectly content to absorb life rather than comment on it, and after awhile he realized that he liked her, despite her shrewd squint.

She adored Thena, that was obvious in the way she patted and hugged and smiled at her, and Jed could see that the feeling was mutual. It worried him, because he wondered how Thena could leave the ancient black woman, her adopted grandmother, behind. Hell, he'd cart the old gal out to Wyoming and set her up in a fancy house near his and Thena's, if that's what it'd take to make Thena happy.

Thena put the string beans on to cook for dinner. In the interim, Beneba pulled a bottle from her basket and gave Jed a glass of homemade dandelion wine so strong that the huge, unsuspecting swallow he took made his eyes water. "Hah," she snorted, as he blinked rapidly in the wine's aftermath. "His face is red. He wants to cough, but he has too much pride. Maybe that's not a good sign. Too much pride could be his heartbreak."

He'd been tested, and he knew it. "Ma'am, I've had grain alcohol that didn't taste this strong. This stuff would burn the hide off a full-grown elephant. Pride's got nothin' to do with my not coughin'. My lungs are shriveled up."

She laughed, obviously considering that a compliment, and afterwards squinted at him with a degree of approval, he thought. They ate a dinner of new potatoes, fried fish, cornbread, and the fresh-cooked beans, then sat on the porch again and watched twilight cover the moss-draped forest with mysterious shadows. Beneba smoked her pipe and pumped herself back and forth in the largest of Thena's four rockers. Thena sat in one next to her, and Jed settled at Thena's feet. She stroked his hair affectionately, and he leaned against her bare legs with sleepy devotion.

He wore only the white pants, but wished he wore nothing at all, so that every inch of his body could bask in the warm, caressing air. If Beneba hadn't been visiting, he and Thena would be sitting here naked. Nakedness—"nekkidness," as Thena said when she imitated him—was their accustomed state on many occasions, both in and out of bed.

But for now, Thena wore floppy blue shorts and a 1950s bathing suit top that had belonged to her mother. Its rigid modesty didn't suit her, he thought, but its innocence did. He smiled with a sense of peace and happiness that swelled his chest.

"You," Beneba told him abruptly, "are a blessed man. I see it on your face. I hear it in the rhythm of your breath. This place has taken your heart."

Jed looked up into her sharp, wise eyes. "No," he corrected politely. He wasn't going to risk Yoda's wrath, but he wasn't going to listen to any mumbo jumbo about the island, either. He nodded toward Thena. "This woman has taken my heart." Her fingers pressed deeply into his hair in loving response.

"Thena and the island are the same. You love one, you love the other." Beneba let pipe smoke curl lazily toward the porch rafters. "You leave one, you leave the other."

Jed frowned uneasily. "I'm not gonna leave Thena."

"You will leave Sancia, and you will leave Thena. I have dreamed it."

Jed cursed silently as Thena's fingers stiffened against his scalp. "What makes you say such an awful thing, Grandmother?" she demanded.

"Because it's true, child. Your man won't admit that he has taken this place into his heart. He'll make himself leave one day, because he's stubborn and full of blind hate for his grandfather. I can only pray that he'll be smart enough to come back."

"You don't mince words, do you," Jed said in a stern voice. He leaned forward and hooked his arms around his updrawn knees, his blissful mood ruined. "But you don't know me well enough to tell my future."

"I know you. I know what you come from, because I was your mother's nursemaid."

Both Jed and Thena looked at her in shock. "You never told me, Grandmother," Thena murmured numbly. "Why not?"

The thin shoulders shrugged. "Old memories are best saved for appropriate times. I saved this one for this moment." Her ghostly eyes bored into Jed's. "I watched your mother being born. I helped raise her. Hardly a day went by for ten years that she and I weren't together. Ten years, until your grandmother was killed in the hurricane. Then your grandfather cursed this island to hell and took your mother away with him."

Her eyes gleamed in a way that made goose bumps run up Jed's arms. "And now you're here to complete the circle," she added. "You can bring back hope; you can lift the curse." She paused, her aura so hypnotizing that even the night insects seemed to have stopped singing, to listen. "I want to see your mother's grandchildren grow up here. Your children. Yours and Thena's."

Jed's stomach twisted in anger. "This island isn't some sort of magical shrine, and I've had all I can take hearin' about it. No child of mine and Thena's is gonna grow up here in the shadow of old man Gregg's dreams. He doesn't deserve that kind of honor."

"Jedidiah?" Thena whispered in a bewildered, wounded tone. "Is Beneba right? Are you going to leave?"

He twisted around and slowly grasped one of her hand in his. Even in the dimming light, he could read the fear in her silver eyes. Jed fought to make his voice sound light and teasing. "Now, gal, do you really think an island is the right place for a quarter horse ranch?"

She stared at him desperately. "There's plenty of room here for your horses, Jedidiah. Sancia is six miles long, remember. It's huge. And—"

"And it's beautiful, I know. It'll always be beautiful, and we'll enjoy it every time we come to visit."

"Visit? You mean you want me to live somewhere else?"

"I want you to live in Wyoming. We'll take the dogs and Cendrillon and any of the other horses you want." Her hand was cold and trembling. He grasped it harder, urgency gnawing at him. Again he tried to sound lighthearted. "Sweetheart, all the spirits you believe in here—they're your spirits, not mine. They'd just as soon spit in my eye as look at me."

"Your grandfather loved your mother," Beneba interjected. "He loved you. He didn't do by halves—he loved with all his soul. I saw that, time and time again, for years, and I know you judge him too harshly. He was a stubborn man—that I know too. He made mistakes. But he would never let his child, his little Amanda, die. If he had known she needed help—"

"He drove her away, he didn't ask how she got along, he didn't want to know, he let her die," Jed said curtly. "Then he tried to take me away from my old man, who—God knows—didn't have anything left but me."

Thena stroked Jed's hand anxiously. Her voice was tearful and begging. "Don't you see, Jedidiah, that you were all your grandfather Gregg had left too? He wanted his little grandson, who was the only bit of Amanda and Sarah who still lived. He loved you."

Jed pulled his hand away from hers and stood up. The light was nearly gone now, and the night was turning as black as his anger. He paced the porch, his hands clenched. "And when he couldn't get me on his own terms, we never heard from him again. That shows how damn little he really cared."

Beneba's voice was calm and low. "Wyoming State Rodeo Association, Junior All-Around Champion, 1974," she recited. Jed stopped pacing and looked at her in tense surprise. Thena, bewildered too, watched Beneba silently.

"How did you know that about me?" Jed asked the elderly woman.

She blinked slowly and let more pipe smoke waft upward before she answered. "Your grandfather didn't forget his little girl's nanny. He left me some money and some treasures—picture albums and scrapbooks about Amanda. And Amanda's son." She paused to concentrate on rocking for a moment. "Every time you got your name in the paper for anything, your grandfather knew it. You goin' rodeo in Texas and get written in the paper there, he gets a copy. You goin' rodeo in Canada and get written in the paper there, he gets a copy. I think he pays somebody just to keep track of what you do in the world." She puffed her pipe again and tilted her little face up impishly. "You come to my house anytime, I'll show you the picture books."

Jed stared at her speechlessly, his jaw working. "I didn't know," Thena murmured beside him. "Grandmother, you should have told me."

"I waited to tell Jed, first. I know when the time is right."

Jed tried to regain control of his emotions. He walked to the edge of the porch and stood with his back turned, one hand braced on a rough-hewn column that supported the roof. Thena rose and went to him, her heart aching. She studied his expression fervently, trying to read it in the dark.

Behind them, Beneba recited other milestones in Jed's rodeo career—not an illustrious career, but one that had gotten his name mentioned in dozens of small papers across the western United States. It was odd to hear Beneba using terms such as "bull dogging" and "bronc riding," Thena thought with nervous humor.

Thena touched Jed's shoulder. "We should go see these scrapbooks," she urged gently. "They'll change your mind about your grandfather. He must have loved you so."

An eternity passed before he looked at her. "Nothin'," Jed told her in a deadly, slow voice, "is ever goin' to change what happened to my mother. He waited too long to do anything decent. She was already dead."

Thena was careful not to sound rebuking. "She was too proud to ask for help, Jedidiah. You said so yourself, once."

"Because he was so against her for marryin' my pa. Can you blame her for not crawlin' to her daddy after the way he'd acted about the marriage?"

"But he would have helped her, Jedidiah. That's the point. Despite everything, he would have helped her. He doesn't deserve so much anger on your part."

He sighed and gently placed one square, rough hand against her cheek. His thumb caressed the soft skin with tender care. "I gave you this island, Thena. Believe me, I had to give up a lot of my anger when I did that."

"I know, and I'm proud of you. Now give up the rest."

"I hear what you're sayin' about old Gregg really bein' sorry for what happened. Maybe it's so and maybe it isn't." He paused. "I'm more worried about your feelin's for this island than I am about the mysterious brand of love—whatever it was—my grandpa had for my mother and me."

"You don't have to be worried about my feelings, Jedidiah. Just stay here and—"

"Sweetheart, I can't live here. I haven't got it in me to love this place the way you do. Maybe I feel like I'm trespassin' on Gregg property."

"But you're a Gregg," she said in a beseeching tone.

"No, I'm not. I might have the blood, but not the background. I don't belong here."

"You do, you do. Jedidiah, this place is where I belong, you know that. How can you ask me to leave it?"

He rebuked her, but gently. "Gal, you haven't ever seen anything else of the world. You don't know what's out there on the mainland. There are other places you'd love just as well as this."

"No." Her voice trembled with controlled sorrow. "My parents and Nate died because they went to the mainland. I have a bad knee because I went to the mainland. People there are too hurried, too interested in unimportant things—"

"Things that aren't important to you, you mean," he prodded in his soft-spoken but firm way. His hand still cupped her face, trying to soothe her. "You gotta visit my world, sweetheart. Don't you think that's only fair? Just to see how things really are outside of your *National Geographics*?"

Thena felt like a trapped bird. Her pulse racing, she whispered, "I'm afraid, Jedidiah."

"I know, pretty lady, but I won't let anything bad happen to you. Will you go—for a visit, at least?"

Beneba's soft voice interrupted him. "Tasoneela go with Gabel, and he brought her back when she was unhappy. Will you do the same for Thena?"

Jed's eyes locked on Thena's. "Yes," he promised.

Thena spoke wistfully. "How long will we have to stay in Wyoming?"

"Sweetheart, we won't just go to Wyoming. We'll go all sorts of places. Wherever you'd like to go. Anyplace you've dreamed about."

"Go, child," Beneba ordered smugly. "I'll look out for your animals. You should see other places, because then you'll come back loving your island even more. And maybe, if your man is smart, he'll come back with you. I hope so."

Thena's eyes shut tightly. She swayed a tiny bit, and Jed took her in this arms. "You'll have so much fun you'll wonder why you never wanted to travel before," he assured her.

"I'm really ignorant about some things, Jedidiah. I've never ridden on a plane, I've never been in an elegant restaurant, I've never seen a big city. . . ."

"Well, gal, I'm not Cary Grant, but I got the worldly

smarts to take care of anything that might come up. Relax." She placed both hands on his bare chest and tilted her head back, looking thoughtful and distressed. "Now tell me some places you've always wanted to visit," he urged.

Tentative enthusiasm tinged her voice. "Disneyland?"

He chuckled. "All right. Where else?"

Her eyes widened. "Hollywood?"

"Shoot, yeah!" He exhaled in relief. "I was afraid you'd say someplace weird."

Beneba's voice, dry and flat, came to them. "I read the *National Enquirer*. Hollywood is weird."

Jed shook his head in amusement. "Enquiring Yoda's want to know," he deadpanned under his breath. To Thena he said, "We'll rent a big ol' car, drive to Atlanta, and get on a plane for California. After we visit there a few days, we'll go to Wyoming for a week or so." His eyes flickered with sudden inspiration. "Let's go ahead and leave tomorrow. I don't want you sittin' around here frettin' over it. The sooner we go, the better."

"Tomorrow?" She began to shake. He held her tighter and pressed her head to his shoulder.

"You'll love it," he crooned.

"I'm doing this because I love you, Jedidiah. I'd never leave Sancia otherwise."

"Not even for two weeks? Two itty bitty weeks? Lord, woman, you're a tough cookie to crumble."

"You want me to stay away from Sancia forever."

He ignored a guilt pang. "Aw, gal, I never said that. I love you too much to ask you to do that. I just want you to give my world a chance before you make up your mind about where's the best place to live."

Jed pressed his cheek to her forehead and shut his eyes as he absorbed the dear and familiar scent of her, the feel of her clinging to him, and the way her heart pattered against his chest. Concern for her made him feel a nauseating dread that he couldn't define.

A suffocating tension caught his breath. It made no sense, this feeling. The bile rose in his throat as he tried to understand where such an odd . . . almost a premonition . . . came from. God, no, he thought quickly, fearfully. It wasn't a premonition. He didn't believe in premonitions.

Craziness, that's what this feeling was. The pull of this damn fairy-tale place with its old mansion and Thena's talk of spirits and Beneba's bizarre eyes. What had happened to his practical, sensible nature? The ugly sensation of dread passed, and he shivered as if recovering from a bad fever. His stomach relaxed and he could breathe again. There, that was better. What the hell had happened to him for a moment?

"Jedidiah? Love?" Thena's pained and frightened voice pierced his thoughts. She was gasping for breath. "You're holding me too tight, Jedidiah. How can I travel if I have crushed ribs?"

Showing Thena the world was going to be a unique experience, Jed decided with a rueful smile. On the drive up to Atlanta, she played with every button, knob, and lever in the ritzy Oldsmobile he had rented. When they stopped for lunch at the Dixie Dog Restaurant and Gift Shop, she spotted a display of the tacky coconut heads that plagued every tourist trap on the interstate.

She loved them. Jed was dumbfounded, but eager to please her, so he bought her two of the ugly things and winced when the cashier cheerfully pointed out that they were the first people to buy coconut heads since a tour bus full of Kiwanians had passed through, and that was six months ago.

And further up the highway, at a convenience store, she bought a copy of a glitzy women's magazine named *Lovers*. She bent her head over the glossy pages and read solemnly as he drove.

Jed was suddenly aware of her nimble fingers tickling the inside of his denimed thigh. She was still reading, her face a mask of concentration. He glanced at her, tried to ignore her for at least five minutes, but finally gave into the wonderful heat that spread outward from her unexpected caress.

"Lord, gal, what are you tryin' to do?"

"It says here that you're supposed to like this."

"I do, but not at sixty miles an hour."

"People do this all the time, it says here." Still reading, her attitude serious and clinical, she unzipped his jeans and began sliding her hand inside. "Now I'll just—oh, my, I don't have to do anything, do I." *Lovers* fell to the floor and her gaze darted to his lap. Her fingers stroked the magnificent result of their bold invasion. "Jedidiah," she whispered throatily. "Jedidiah, that magazine is very informative."

His eyes were half-closed, his breathing a little shallow. "Did it tell you what happens next, Miss Witch?"

"Uhmmm, no, I hadn't got to that part yet. I can . . . make a logical deduction, however."

He pulled off at the next exit and found a dirt road that took them to the middle of nowhere. Then he cut the engine and slid across the seat, his eyes daring her deliciously, his hands already reaching for her legs. Thena smiled breathlessly at the impatient hunger with which he captured her. His hands pushed her sundress off her shoulders and rubbed her bare breasts, her thighs, her stomach, skimming waves of pleasure across her skin, making her feel wild and tender and greedy all at once.

"I'd love to keep going," he murmured in a gravelly voice. "But we better not. Not here."

Thena raked her hands through his hair and made a soft, plaintive sound. "I love you, Jedidiah. I want you."

"I love you, too . . . now don't go doin' that . . . don't coax me like that . . . oh, gal, you win."

When they finally got back on the highway, Jed drove with one hand and put his other arm around her shoulders. Both of them were smiling and quiet. Eventually he said in a droll voice, "Thena, I'm gonna buy you a subscription to that magazine."

The cavernous terminal of Atlanta's ultramodern international airport left her speechless. As Jed waited at one of the car rental counters to return the Olds, he let his eyes flicker protectively to where she stood studying the selections on a newsstand. His gaze softened every time he looked at her, because she was so beautiful and so unaware of it.

She wore her lacy sundress with sandals and a delicate white sweater that emphasized the billowing dark mane of hair down her back. Men eyed her with open intrigue, and Jed frowned in surprise. Of course he'd always known that she was too beautiful and exotic not to draw attention from other men, but he'd never had to deal with that fact on Sancia. He shifted, impatient to finish with the car chore and get back beside her.

He watched as she flinched at the beeping alert of a small courtesy shuttle and turned around to stare. As the shuttle rolled past her, she raised one hand and waved tentatively at the man who drove it. He smiled and nodded. She smiled and nodded.

Jed shook his head in gentle amusement. This was like that movie, *Crocodile Dundee*, about the naive Australian who visited New York City. At baggage check-in, Thena had politely asked the clerk when he was going to examine her suitcase for drugs and bombs. He gave her a long, straight-faced appraisal, then said almost to himself, "Naaaah," and handed her a claim check. Jed led her away quickly. Next, she'd noticed a man using a bank teller machine and wondered if the airport had installed a game that gave prize money. Then she'd asked Jed if the two of them could hurry so they'd be first in line to board their plane. She wanted to beat the rush for the best seats.

The car clerk spoke to Jed, taking his attention. When he finished with the clerk and turned toward the newsstand again, Thena had disappeared. Jed halted, his heart jerking with alarm as he scanned the terminal. Relief made his knees weak when he located Thena at a small booth near the concourse escalators. She was talking amicably to an orange-robed man with a shaved head. The man seemed utterly delighted.

His expression determined and his attitude firm, Jed strolled over to the booth. She looked up excitedly. "This is a follower of Krishna, Jedidiah. We're discussing the Bhagavad Gita. I love it. It's a fascinating Sanskrit poem." She looked back at the man. "What a novel way for you to seek converts by setting up this booth in the airport. How dedicated."

With an attitude of resignation, Jed retrieved a twenty-dollar bill from his jeans pocket and pressed it into the man's outstretched hand. "Hare Krishna," the man said in thanks.

"Mmmm. Holy moly." Then he took Thena's arm and guided her away. She waved good-bye to her new friend, then looked at Jed, her eyes gleaming with amazement.

"Why did you give him money?"

"That's what he's there for, sweetheart. That's why he talks to people. Since you liked his poetry, I reckoned you'd like to contribute to his cause, whatever it is."

She was silent, pondering such an exploitative enterprise on the man's part. "My goodness," she whispered, stunned. "Talk isn't cheap on the mainland, is it?"

He chuckled. "That's all right, Miss Dundee, I've got plenty of money, and you're welcome to use it in any way that makes you happy." He paused. "Except you can't buy any more of those durned coconut heads."

"Miss Dundee?"

He put his arm around her. "Never mind. The point is, I want you to have a good time. I don't want you to feel bad about leavin' the island for one minute."

Jed had never really blessed his extraordinary wealth before, but now he did. It seemed fitting that his grandfather's money should be used to make Thena happy. She was, after all, the heart and soul of the island old Gregg had once loved. Fancy rental cars, first-class airline seats, a California shopping spree to buy Thena whatever caught her eye—these luxuries were what she deserved, and Jed intended to provide them.

As they sat in their plush airplane seats, waiting to taxi, Thena clutched Jed's strong, warm hand and looked out the window, fighting tears. She loved him, and she was going to give his complicated world a fair chance.

Then, like Tasoneela and Gabel, they were going to come back where they belonged.

Eleven

Noise. Confusion. Crowds. Mickey Mouse. Thena glued wistful eyes to the giant cartoon character, seeking comfort for her jangled nerves. He waved to the sweaty mass of humanity and smiled his manufactured, frozen smile as he paraded down the studiously quaint Disneyland street.

People bumped into Thena in their attempts to secure a good view of him, their cameras poking her arms, their drinks sloshing dangerously near her new outfit—pink twill shorts with a snug white belt, a blue polo shirt, and pristine white Reeboks. She wasn't fond of the clothes, but the saleslady at the fashionable store had told her and Jed that they were just right for Disneyland. Her new bra, a necessity under the clingy shirt, was itchy and confining. She shifted nervously.

Confinement was a way of life on the mainland, it seemed. She'd never seen so many buildings crammed onto such small pieces of land. People liked to stay inside here; they preferred their air-conditioning to the outdoor air. She had to agree that the air smelled and tasted bad. In fact, if taste had a color, California's air tasted brown. But the luxurious hotel suite Jed had gotten had no windows she could open, and after a few hours locked inside it, she craved air, even brown air, that wasn't still and dry and cold.

On the mainland, pets were as confined as their

owners, and that upset her worst of all. Yesterday, as she and Jed were walking along a street near the hotel, she'd spotted a big dog that resembled Godiva, sitting alone in a parked car at the curb. Worried, Thena put her fingertips on the closed car window and looked directly into the prisoner's eyes, and nothing Jed could say convinced her that the dog wasn't tragically depressed.

In his quiet way, Jed had gotten angry at her stubbornness. She'd sensed that her whimsical notions about animals made him impatient, and she'd barely suppressed her disappointment. Oh, he loved and respected animals—he wasn't a cruel man. But she realized for the first time that he wasn't sentimental about them in the way she was. He was used to making his living from the servitude of animals, after all. They were a business.

The discovery that she didn't know Jed as well as she'd believed had added to her silent melancholy. The discovery that California traffic was terrible had added more. Everyone secluded themselves in cars here, and everyone drove fast. The streets outside the hotel bustled in a way that panicked her, though she never told Jed.

During their first night away from Sancia, she'd suffered a horrible nightmare, the first in more than a year, about the accident that killed Nate and her parents. She awoke shaking, in silent tears, and crept out of bed carefully so she wouldn't wake Jed. She spent the next hour huddled by their room's big window, staring forlornly at the night sky. She would learn to like the mainland, but only for Jed's sake.

Disneyland, oddly enough, was the most confining place of all. Did mainlanders enjoy waiting in long lines for everything? she wondered. They waited patiently, but as they waited, they gripped their cameras and umbrellas and handbags with a possessiveness she couldn't fathom. Why, no one would steal from a person at Disneyland, would they?

Mickey Mouse fans closed in on her, blocking her line of vision, their colognes, perfumes, and suntan lotions a cloying combination. Suddenly claustrophobia and homesickness overwhelmed her. But she couldn't leave this spot, because Jed, who'd gone to get them both a soft drink, would never find her again, and the idea of being lost from him in this crazy, frightening wonderland made her tremble.

She couldn't, she shouldn't—a large, thick-faced young man in a tank top and tight jeans leaned over and leered, "Hey, sweet mama, if you got the time, I got the place"—and she bolted.

Thena pushed her way through the huge crowd until she reached a water fountain. She clung to it, white-knuckled, as if an inanimate object was the only friend she could find.

"Thena!" She looked around frantically and spotted Jed easing through the crowd toward her. Even he wasn't familiar, she thought in despair. Dark designer sunglasses hid his eyes, and he wore crisp white tennis shorts, a white Izod shirt, and white Reeboks similar to hers. Rich, sleek, incredibly handsome—he was all of those likeable things, but she wanted her dusty cowboy back.

He frowned as he reached the water fountain. "Woman, this ain't the right time for you to get the itch to wander." She relaxed a little at the sound of his low, teasing growl. Jed would always be Jed—loving, dear, and concerned.

"Oh," she answered in a voice that strained for lightness, "I just felt a little too hot. I needed a drink of water."

"You okay, wildflower?" He handed her a tall paper cup full of ice and soft drink, then slipped an arm around her shoulders.

"Sure." Her head bobbed in something resembling an enthusiastic nod.

"Did you get a good gander at the fake mouse?" He'd never admit to being fascinated by a cartoon mouse himself, she thought with gentle amusement, and his cynical choice of words showed that.

"Yes, indeed. He's very cute."

"How about some lunch?"

"Is there . . . is there a quiet place somewhere . . ."

"Your face is white, gal. Are you feelin' sick?"

Sick, scared, and depressed, yes. "I'm okay."

"Thena." His tone rebuked her gently. "Have you seen all you can take of this place? Tell the truth." She nodded, looking defeated. "Come on, gal." He steered her through the crowd, using his body to block a path for her.

Tenderness and gratitude mingled inside her. "I love you, Jedidiah," she said fervently. "You're trying so hard to take care of me."

"Are you havin' a good time, darlin'?"

"Oh, yes. But I think I'd like to visit Hollywood sooner than we intended. Could we drive up this afternoon?" She needed a dose of romantic glamour; she knew she'd feel better if she could just visit the source of all her beloved old movies.

"Anything you want, sweetheart. We'll just pack up and mosey along to Hollywood, then."

She smiled crookedly and sighed with relief. "Head 'em up and move 'em out."

Greer Garson and Barbara Stanwyck gleamed, but most everyone else, including her idol, Judy Garland, was dirty. Thena sadly studied the stars' names on the sidewalk plaques, then looked up and studied Hollywood's most famous intersection with even more sorrow. Hollywood and Vine, the place of her fanciful dreams, was tacky and run-down.

And the people who frequented it weren't the stuff stars were made of, she thought, unless one was casting for bums, winos, criminal types, and loitering young women with an odd manner of peering in the windows of stopped cars. Earlier she'd asked Jed what the women meant by such rude behavior.

He shook his head at her naïveté and surveyed her with mild astonishment. "They're doin' man business," he said gently. "You savvy what I mean?"

"Ah. Ah, yes." Her eyes narrowed in concentration.

"Don't look at 'em like you just discovered a new breed of sea turtle and you gotta check it out," he warned in a droll voice. "If you wander over there and talk to one of 'em, I'm not payin' her twenty bucks—not even if she's a Hare Krishna on the side."

Thena shook her head wearily. She didn't want to get any closer to mainland sadness than she already had. "I'm going to look for Rudolph Valentino," she announced, and meandered down the sidewalk.

"Well, just don't look in any car windows for him."

There were 1,844 star plaques in the sidewalks, Thena's tourist brochure said. Jed worked his way in the opposite direction from her, searching for John Wayne. Thena found Rudolph's star and studied it earnestly. A whooshing sound caught her attention, and she glanced up.

Thena gasped, shocked to see a wretched-looking old woman down on all fours scrubbing one of the plaques with a soapy rag. Her stained polyester pantsuit looked like a good candidate for rag status itself. Her hair was cut as close as a man's, and her scrawny face was an accordian of wrinkles. She was as impoverished and ugly as the buildings behind her. Thena walked over to the woman and knelt down, her heart overflowing with sympathy.

"Can I help you wash that?" she asked pleasantly.

Rheumy old eyes, suspicious and mean, glared up at her. "Beat it, you pandhandler."

Thena blinked swiftly, and her face colored. "I don't want any money. I want to help."

The old voice rose to a curdling shriek. "Clark

Gable's all I got left, and nobody washes his star but me!" Her shrillness stabbed at Thena's senses. "Especially not a foreigner!"

Thena stood, mortified. Foreigner? Did her odd accent—Southern and slightly French—mark her as even more of an outsider? Footsteps hurried up behind her.

"What's the problem?" Jed asked, as he angled himself between her and the woman's violent glare. Thena looked around in chagrin. Other people were staring at her, and a pair of teenage boys with spikes set in their hair—wait a second, those spikes *were* their hair—snickered with unconcealed enjoyment as they strode past. Thena whispered urgently, "Give me some money, Jedidiah, please."

He arched one brow in surprise, but handed her a twenty. She held it out to the woman. "Will you wash Judy Garland's star for me?"

Jed understood Thena's kind motive and quickly handed her another twenty. "And John Wayne's too," he said.

A bony hand snapped forward and snatched the bills from Thena. "Yeah. The Duke and Judy. Got it." The voice was still loud and resentful.

"Thank you," Thena murmured. She pivoted and grabbed Jed's arm, her eyes glistening with tears. "Can we go back to the hotel?"

He surveyed the disillusionment in her eyes and winced at her pain. He knew that the first few days of their trip had been a stressful, unpleasant experience for her. "It'll get better, sweetheart," he said with quiet, desperate firmness.

Her fingers dug into his arm. "Please. Please, can we go back to the hotel?"

"You're not bein' fair, Thena. . . ."

"If you won't take me," she said emphatically. "I'll go on my own."

She saw the exasperation and worry rising behind

his hazel eyes, as well as the annoyance. His voice was low and tight. "Fine. We'll go hide, if that's what you want."

That hurt, and she shot him an accusing, wounded look. They turned silently, not touching, and walked toward the car.

They had a plush hotel room near Beverly Hills. It was late afternoon when they arrived there, and low rays of sunlight angled through a pair of magnificent louvered windows to make patterns on the king-size bed.

"I'm going to take a nap," Thena murmured. She lay down on the thick, satiny coverlet and looked over her shoulder at Jed, her heart twisting with unhappiness. Except for a few quiet, neutral words, they hadn't spoken since walking to the car. Anger hung in the air, bitter and black. Jed lowered himself into a fat, contemporary-style armchair and opened a copy of *Tom Sawyer*, one she'd given him.

Weary and depressed, Thena put a hand out and closed it around the patterned, golden sunshine that washed across the bed, thinking of the way the afternoon rays always turned Sancia's western shores into a blaze of color. She drew her hand next to her face as if she were bringing sunshine and hope close to her. Comforted, she dozed.

Jed sat very still, his eyes burning as he considered her wistful gesture. She hurts, he thought sadly. She wants to go home. What the hell am I going to do? A minute later, he went over to the bed, lay down close to her, and cupped his body to her back and hips. He curled an arm around her waist and gently buried his face in her hair. She sighed softly and snuggled against him in a way that made the earlier anger evaporate from his thoughts.

"I love you," he whispered. Even in sleep she must have heard, because her hand sought his and snugly intertwined their fingers. One corner of Jed's mouth lifted in a pensive smile as he fell asleep beside her in the sunshine.

Thena awoke an hour later. She ruffled Jed's hair and kissed his mouth tenderly. He stirred. "Hmmm."

"Jedidiah, I'm going downstairs to the gift shop and look at the magazines. I'll be right back."

"Hmmm." He nodded groggily.

Downstairs, Thena wandered idly along an arched, marbled hallway that fronted expensive boutiques, eyeing the colorful and bizarre clothes on the window mannequins. *"Sacrebleu!"* she said out loud. *"Dispendieux et laid comme un crapaud!"*

A high-pitched male laugh startled her. Thena looked down the hall to a shop entrance several doors further. A lanky, fair-skinned man in designer jeans and a feminine-looking, canary-yellow shirt smiled at her warmly.

"Expensive and ugly as sin!" he echoed, in English. "My dear, I adore your description of those tawdry rags!"

Intrigued because he looked so different from any man she'd ever met before, Thena smiled back. A gleaming art nouveau doorway in black and gold framed him. Above his head, scrawled in ornate neon letters, a sign said simply, Tresses. She looked back at the man, who was still smiling.

"Oooh," he sighed slowly. "That lovely, unstructured hair of yours. What miracles I could work with that." Another man, just as feminine-looking and just as friendly, poked his head out the door and studied her. A long cigarette was posed elegantly in the man's fingertips.

"Remarkable," the second man crooned. "What texture. What thickness. She reminds one of an unstructured Kathleen Turner, doesn't she?"

Thena touched her shaggy brunet hair. What was this "unstructured" business and why did it sound vaguely uncomplimentary? She wanted to make Jed happy. She wanted to fit in on the mainland. Perhaps by becoming structured she'd have a better chance. "You cut hair?" she asked politely.

Both the lanky man and his companion laughed. Thena puzzled over them, then decided she liked them. They were exotic. She was exotic, too, and they seemed to appreciate that fact. The lanky man swept into a low bow.

"Monsieur Markus, the proprietor, at your service, mademoiselle."

"Merci," she answered, and curtsied. More laughter.

"Mademoiselle, I do, as you say, cut hair. But don't tell anyone. My clients expect to have their hair 'designed,' not cut."

Thena walked toward his salon. "Would you design my hair? I'm staying here at the hotel," she hurried to add, "and I can afford whatever you charge." Jedidiah will be so pleased with my mainland look, she thought in excitement.

Monsieur Markus chewed his lower lip and tugged at his smooth jaw with long, cool-looking fingers as he appraised her hair. Then he nodded, his eyes gleaming with plans. "Come into my salon, said the spider to the fly." He winked wickedly and gestured toward the interior. Her whole body tingling with expectation, Thena walked inside.

When Jed woke up, the sunlight had been replaced by long evening shadows. The big hotel room was dark except for lines of light that escaped around the edges of the closed bathroom door. The sounds of muffled crying—he heard them and knew they were the reason he'd wakened. Thena's crying. Jed leapt off the bed, rushed to the bathroom door, and shoved it open.

Sitting on the side of the sunken whirlpool tub, her head hidden under a huge beige towel, Thena looked up in tearful shock. Immediately, she composed her face and wrenched a smile from some determined recess of her soul. "Oh . . . oh, hello, Jedidiah. I just finished reading a sad, sad magazine story, and . . ."

He knelt in front of her and grasped her tear-streaked face between his hands. She clutched the towel tight under her chin, and Jed's eyes filled with concern at such a strange, secretive reaction. "Sweetheart, what's wrong? What the hell kind of story makes you cry and hide in the john with your head under a towel?"

"Oh . . . it was about . . . Madonna and Sean Penn. She's a singer of some sort, you see, and he's an actor, and they're married. He's constantly hitting people, and it's very romantic, and—"

"Thena," Jed said in a warning tone. He tried to ease the towel off her head, but she pulled away from his grasp. A sob tore from her lips as she buried her face against his shoulder, the towel still over her head.

"The truth," he commanded. She made a small keening sound of despair.

"I had my hair designed, Jedidiah! I went downstairs . . . there was this beauty parlor called Tresses, and the owner spoke French—"

"Are you sayin' you got your hair cut off?"

The horrified tone of his voice sent her into a crying spasm that soaked a large spot on his cotton polo shirt. Not only was she distressed by what she'd done, but Jedidiah obviously hated the idea—even the idea—of her getting her hair cut. Oh, no.

"Sweetheart, sweetheart, ssssh." He tried to tease, for her sake. "What'd you do? Get a crew cut?" His eyes clouded with alarm, he quickly held her away from him and pulled the towel off her head. His involuntary gasp and pained grimace spoke volumes.

"I'm sorry, Jedidiah! I didn't know a hair design would be so short!" She snatched the towel back and buried her face in it, her shoulders shaking.

After a moment he calmly pried her face up from the towel and grasped it between his callused, loving hands. Her once-glorious mane of hair now lay in feathery, gently curving layers that ended just below her ears. It gave her a sophisticated, pert appearance that was very appealing. But he had loved her long hair.

"Why?" he groaned. "Why did you do it? I thought you liked your hair."

"I did, but I thought getting it cut would . . . please you. I wanted to make up for being such an uncooperative toad earlier today." She shivered, biting her lip to contain a new round of sobs. Jed took her in his arms and held her tightly.

"My poor baby. What have I done to you by haulin' you off to this damned place? Sssh. I love you. I like your hair," he lied, "It's real short, but pretty."

"I look like a mare who's had her mane roached."

"Quiet down now. Hush, sweetheart."

He carried her to the bed, stripped off her clothes, and put her under the covers. Then he got a wet washcloth and gently dabbed at her swollen face. She grew still and silent, her sad, silver eyes following him, never leaving him. He ordered sumptuous lobster dinners and a bottle of champagne from room service and switched the room's television to a showing of *Jane Eyre* with Orson Welles.

Her eyes widened with interest, and she looked a little happier. When room service arrived, Jed undressed and got in bed with her, and they ate off bed trays. The champagne eased her misery, and by the time she finished dessert, she could bear to crane her neck and look at herself in the dresser mirror across from their bed.

Jane Eyre caused her to cry again, and Jed was grateful when it ended. Thena's tears made him admit that nothing would be right until she was back on Sancia. He turned the television and lights off, then slid back in bed, his heart aching and worried. She came to him in the dark, her arms warm and comforting, as if she knew that the last few days had been hell for him too.

"Sweet man," she whispered. "Sweet, caring man. Be still and let me care for you now."

She pulled the covers back, exposing his naked body to her hands and mouth. Lying on his back, Jed moaned softly as a powerful combination of love and desire tugged at his senses. Thena was as all-encompassing as the darkness; she aroused every inch of his skin, kissing the scars and the calluses with the same devotion that she gave to the more alluring parts of his body.

It seemed that she caressed him for hours, but her hands never tired of their sensuous waltz over his stomach and thighs, then up to his shoulders, then across his throat and down to his nipples, where they paused each time to swirl his curly hair and approve the swift rising and falling of his chest.

When she concentrated her attention on his most sensitive place, he pressed his head back into the pillow and whispered her name like a prayer. His big, ordinarily calm hands weren't calm any longer. They hung in the air, quivering, then stroked her hair and followed the highly erotic rhythm of her movements.

Thena was the other half of his soul and his dreams, as inseparable from him as night from day. It was dangerous to be this close to another person, he knew—it left him open for more hurt than he'd ever known was possible. But that wasn't important compared to the fulfillment and happiness she gave him with her touch, her voice, her love.

A bittersweet emotion caused a knot in the pit of his stomach. The future was a dark place on the horizon because he knew she belonged on Sancia, and he didn't. He had spent too many years hating his grandfather to change completely; the ugly feeling would always be with him, a discordant note that would destroy the island's harmony—his and Thena's harmony—if he tried to live there.

His eyes shut fiercely tight, his teeth clenched, Jed cried out as he rose to meet the incessant invitation of her mouth and hands. He collapsed back on the bed, his breathing harsh and unsteady.

She quickly covered him and took him in her arms, cradling his head against her breasts. Her hands stroked his damp hair with alarm. "Jedidiah, it's all right," she soothed, her voice worried. "I won't leave you."

"What . . . why are you sayin' that?" he gasped raggedly. He knew he'd spoken words a moment earlier, but they'd been forgotten in his haze of heartache and release.

"You said . . . 'don't go.' " Her voice broke. "I won't, Jedidiah, I won't—"

"You have to," he said in anguish. "You don't belong on the mainland."

"No, I do belong! I belong wherever you are—"

"I'll visit you, and you'll visit me. We'll make do—"

She put a hand over his mouth to silence him. She held him with desperate possessiveness, her head bent low over his, her lips pressed into his hair. "No more talk tonight," she begged in a thready, barely audible voice. "I don't want to talk about it. I want to go to Wyoming tomorrow."

He nuzzled his face against her and placed a kiss on the silky skin over her heart. "No more talk," he promised wearily. There was no need. The issue was settled, and they both knew it.

Their horses stood quietly, ears relaxed and eyes droopy, as the crisp September wind swept down from the white mountains and whirled across the prairie to their place on the high, grassy knoll.

Thena reached down distractedly and stroked her bay's warm neck. "Wyoming is a beautiful place, Jedidiah," she said sincerely. "The air tastes wonderful here. It tastes . . . blue."

Beside her on a tall roan, Jed's mouth curved in a tired smile. Whimsy and small talk, that's what she wanted. They'd been pretending for the past two days, ever since that emotional night in California, that everything was just wonderful.

"A thousand acres," he murmured, gesturing at the land in front of them, "and it'll all be mine if I just sign my name to a piece of paper." He paused, letting the wind sift through the enormity of that idea. "It's what I've dreamed about all my life, havin' land like this."

"I know, sweetheart, I know. Your ranch. Your dream. I understand."

Sorrow cut through him as if the wind had just seeped between his bones. Jed closed his eyes a moment, gathering strength. When he opened them, he stared straight ahead, seeking the mountains as a focus.

"I'll build whatever kind of house you like best," he told her in a desperately calm voice. "So when you're here, you'll feel at home. You can buy whatever makes you happy, to go in it."

She reached over and clasped his hand tightly. He turned his head slowly, his gaze painfully controlled, to look at her. The gaze she returned was both loving and troubled.

"And whatever you want done to the house on Sancia, I'll do it," she told him. "So that when you're there, you'll feel at home."

He nodded. "Come here, wildflower." In a single, powerful movement, he reached under her arms, lifted her from her horse's back, and pulled her in front of him. The big roan shifted lazily, unconcerned by the new weight. Jed eased back in the saddle so that he could cradle her easily in his arms.

Her eyes glistening, Thena put her hands on his wind-roughened face and drew him to her for a gentle kiss.

"It's time I said the formal thing," he whispered. Their eyes met and held. "Will you marry me?"

She smiled tenderly and answered without hesitation or surprise, just as he had expected. "Yes." They kissed for an eternity, their movements slow and sweet. Without another word, Jed took the reins on Thena's horse and led it beside his as they descended the knoll. Thena rested her face against the crook of Jed's neck, her eyes shut.

More than a mile passed under the horses' hooves before they came to the two-lane state highway where Jed had left a borrowed truck and trailer. They loaded the horses and took them back to the Circle Ten Ranch. Jed's old friends, Mac and Barbara, had loaned them the horses, the vehicles, and a spacious guest room.

That night, Thena made love to Jed for hours in that guest room, and they talked for hours afterward, until they finally fell asleep in each other's arms amidst the jumbled bedcovers. The next morning he climbed into a long-bed stock truck loaded with saddle horses and went with Mac Bullock and a dozen cowboys to a distant part of the ranch to round up cattle. A borrowed jacket pulled tightly around her shoulders, Thena stood by the rear of the truck and smiled up at him.

"I'll be back tonight," he promised, looking a little guilty. "Sure you don't mind?"

"You need to have some fun, Jedidiah, and I know spending the day out on the prairie will make you happy. Go ahead."

He leapt down from the back of the truck and gave her a long kiss, which drew hoots and applause from Mac and his ranch hands. Ignoring them stoically, Jedidiah told her, "Have a good time visitin' with Barbara."

"We're friends already. I'll be fine."

Reassured, he got back in the truck. Thena watched it pull away. Jed hung out the back and tipped his hat to her. It was an old, comfortable-looking tan Stetson that suited him perfectly. The dramatic and dearly loved sight of him in that hat, at home in his world, bolstered her will to do what she had to do next. She waved, her throat on fire with sadness. Then she went back into the Bullocks' big house, where Barbara waited for her, her plump face worried and set.

"You sure?" she asked Thena.

Thena nodded. "I'll be ready to leave in ten minutes."

Twelve

When she arrived back on Sancia, hours later, Thena wearily went through the laborious process of making a long-distance telephone connection via her ham radio. It was four-thirty in the afternoon, her time, but only two-thirty Wyoming time, when she contacted the Circle Ten. She left word with Barbara that she'd call Jed that evening at eight, Wyoming time. He couldn't call her long distance—the telephone/radio connection didn't work in reverse.

The dogs were still with Beneba, and Cendrillon, after galloping to meet her at the dock, had wandered into the forest again. Lonely and depressed, Thena walked the beaches and stared at the horizon—the western horizon always. The years stretched ahead of her and Jed, full of separations such as this. Would the partings always be this difficult? she wondered.

At ten, her hands trembling, she called the Circle Ten a second time. Mac answered the phone and quickly turned it over to Jed, who had obviously been waiting. Thena took a deep breath and tried to ignore the tears that slid slowly down her face.

"Why?" was all he said, but the clipped, anxious word contained a saga of anger and hurt.

"Jedidiah, I decided it was best if I left without telling you—at least this time. You would never have let me come back by myself . . . and I have to learn to travel alone, don't I? And . . . it hurt less, this way."

"You don't know what it did to me, to get back tonight and find out you'd headed across the damn country by yourself." His voice was hard. "It scared the hell out of me."

"I have to learn, my love. You know that."

"Is this how it's going to be when we're married? Will you run for the damn island every time I turn my back?"

"No!"

"I'll be on the first plane to Atlanta in the morning. Dammit, Thena, what you did wasn't fair."

"We agreed that this is the only way we can share a life, Jedidiah. This is how . . . how it's going to be the rest of our lives. We have to get used to it."

"I don't want to get used to it! I want you . . . here." He stopped to compose his voice, which sounded ragged and gruff. "I'll see you tomorrow."

"No." Her tears weren't silent anymore. They invaded her voice and made it waver. "This is the way our life is going to be, Jedidiah. We'll make it wonderful, I promise. But we have to . . . learn to . . . be apart. You can't . . . come. You have to buy your . . . ranch."

"How can I care about a ranch when I'm worried about you on the other side of the country?"

"My spirits look after me, Jedidiah. Don't worry."

"Dammit, Thena, don't talk to me about your spirits. You believe what you want to about spooks, but if you need help, it won't be them who'll know it— it'll be me. That's because there's a bond between two people who love each other as much as we do, and it hasn't got anything to do with any spirits but our own."

"My stubborn Jedidiah." She pressed a hand to her throat, trying to keep her voice from dissolving completely. "I'll call you tomorrow."

"I told you. I'm getting on a plane—"

"To do what? Come here to stay? To live perma-
nently?"

His long silence ended finally in a long stream of
low, tormented curses directed at the madness of
the situation. "No, Jedidiah, you're going to live in
Wyoming and visit Sancia. I'm going to live on Sancia
and visit Wyoming. That's how it will be. I think you
should . . . I think you should come back here . . .
in a month."

"A month?" His voice was tragic.

"I'll call you lots." She heard the incessant buzzing
that signaled that another ham radio operator wanted
to use the phone connection. "Jedidiah. I have to go
now. Promise you won't come here tomorrow. Swear
it."

She thought for several seconds that he wouldn't
answer. Then his low, weary voice rumbled across
the distance. "I swear."

"I love you, Jedidiah."

"Take care of yourself, take good care."

"You too, my love."

They hung on the line, dreading the good-bye.
Another buzz interrupted them. Thena sobbed raggedly. "Good night, cowboy."

"Thena, dear God, Thena."

"Good night, my heart." Then she quickly put her
phone on its cradle by the radio. Thena stumbled to
the bedroom window and sank to the floor by it. She
stared out at the night sky. West.

"Is he hurt bad?" Through a haze of pain, Jed
heard Mac's booming voice and heavy footsteps coming toward him across the training ring. "Damn
crazy man, gettin' on that colt a second time!" Jed
felt Mac's head trainer, Tony Redman, pressing cautious hands over his rib cage. He winced as a dull
ache throbbed through his chest, but forced himself
to sit up.

"No, he's not hurt bad," Jed answered for himself.
He ignored Tony's protests to the contrary and
squinted up at Mac's broad, anxious face. "He's fixin'
to get back on that feisty colt." Across the ring, a
huge gray quarter horse colt snorted derisively and
shook his bridled head.

"The hell you are," Mac informed him. "If you
want to stay here any longer as my guest, you're
gonna calm down and quit takin' risks."

With Mac's and Tony's help, Jed stood up. He
slapped a hand against his dusty leg. "I've been
stomped by tougher colts than this one," he grumbled.

"Yeah, when you were a few years younger and a
helluva lot smarter," Mac retorted. "When you weren't
eaten up with loneliness and worry. These last two
weeks since Thena left, you been worthless. Workin'
twenty hours a day, drinkin' at night, bein' careless—
it's not like you, friend. You gotta cut it out."

Jed shrugged Mac's hand away from his shoulder.
"You want me off the place, I'll go," he offered curtly.

"Oh, yeah? Where? Back to Thena's island? That's
the only place you're gonna be happy. Stop foolin'
yourself, you hardheaded bull."

Jed grasped the older man's hand and looked at
him with a grimace of pain. "I apologize for bein' a
jerk."

"Go back to her, you dumb cowpoke. Go live on
the island."

His chest heaving, Jed straightened wearily. "Can't
do it. The place is no good for me. It's like"— he held
out both hands as if searching for words—"I'm not
wanted there—except by Thena."

Mac's brow furrowed in consternation. "Just who
doesn't want you there? Who else lives there?"

Jed shook his head and ended the discussion with
a tired wave of one hand. If he told Mac that the
island spirits didn't want him there, Mac would give
him a stiff drink and call the doctor. "I'm goin' back

in two weeks," he said. "In the meantime, I'm gonna ride that colt."

He walked toward the arrogant gray, his ribs aching. Jed heard an ominous rattling sound and stopped, his boots frozen to the dusty earth as he scanned the immediate area.

"There's a rattler here," he called over his shoulder. "I can hear it."

The unmistakable warning sound stopped abruptly, but he, Mac, and Tony carefully checked around the outskirts of the ring as well as the benches and water troughs beyond.

"Sun's gettin' to you, man," Mac told him jovially. "There isn't a snake within a mile of this ranch. I didn't hear a thing." He looked at Tony, a short, grizzled man with graying blond hair. "Did you?"

"Me neither, boss." They both looked at Jed curiously.

A little shaken, frowning, Jed passed a hand over his forehead. He'd heard the damn rattlesnake. There was no doubt in his mind. "I think I'll go lie down awhile," Jed said slowly. "I must be punchy."

He turned and walked toward the gate, his eyes dark with bewilderment. The rattling sound started again. This time Jed shivered. "There! Do you hear it now?" he demanded, pivoting around to gaze at the other two men. After a moment of embarrassment, they shook their heads. Jed felt nausea sweep over him. The rattling sound faded, then disappeared entirely. What the hell was going on?

"Call the doc," he told Mac with outward calm. "I must have landed harder than I thought." He swung about and walked toward the gate, fighting an odd feeling of panic that came from nowhere. That wasn't true, he decided after a stricken moment. It came from the horizon. The eastern one.

Jed grabbed the gate with shaking hands. "I'm goin' to the airport," he informed Mac and Tony. "Something's wrong with Thena."

Mac latched a strong grip on his shoulder. "Pardner, you're hurt. Stop it now. Calm down. You're just confused. I think we'll take you on down to doc's, right now."

Jed leaned his head on the gatepost and took several deep breaths. The bad, strange feelings began to fade. This was damn stupid of him, he decided. Mac was right. He was hurt, addled, worn out from lack of sleep and a series of hangovers.

"I'm okay," he promised Mac. "I'll just go lie down. Whew." He shook his head weakly as he raised it. "I must be gettin' old."

"Aren't we all?" Chuckling tensely, Mac guided him toward the main house.

Cold perspiration misted Thena's face and neck. She breathed in shallow, strained gulps as she leaned against the mossy base of a huge oak, studying her swollen right foot. It seemed oddly distant, separate from her body. Whining, Godiva and Rasputin sniffed at the ugly twin puncture marks just above the ankle. They had just finished making certain that the snake that was responsible for those wounds would never again surprise another traveler along this quiet path.

Thena had performed the only immediate first aid possible. She'd torn a thick strip off the skirt of her cotton sundress and tied it tightly above the bite. She knew it was a pitiful excuse for a tourniquet, but perhaps it would keep the venom from weakening her before she could get back to the house and radio for help.

Her head swam, and she touched it fearfully. Thena crawled to her feet, using the oak for support, but dizziness overwhelmed her and she slid down the rough tree trunk with a moan. Her house was on the other side of the island. She'd been taking a shortcut to the northern beach, the beach near SalHaven.

Thena shivered violently. She closed her eyes, struggling to remain clearheaded. She might survive the rattler's venom without medical help, but it was unlikely. She had to get to the house, the radio. She staggered to her feet again, swaying wildly. To her groggy mind, the trees seemed to be full of ethereal whispers. Suddenly Cendrillon trotted up, her eyes wide at the snake smell that still lingered on the balmy air.

"Thank . . . you . . . spirits," Thena murmured. She tried to climb onto Cendrillon, but a sickening blackness accompanied the effort. Thena managed to drape herself over the mare's trembling back, but coherent thought deserted her and she lay immobile there, unable to direct Cendrillon's actions. Unbidden, the mare started to walk, her movements careful and slow.

Minutes, hours, perhaps years later, Thena dimly heard the crisp, hollow sound of Cendrillon's hooves hitting rock. She opened her eyes and squinted down at the ground—no, not ground, marble—the smooth and dingy marble of SalHaven's main hallway. Dull surprise mingled with Thena's lethargic thoughts.

"Why here?" she asked aloud. Her hands swung limply by Cendrillon's front legs as the little mare walked on through the old mansion. A moment later Thena realized that the marble was now dappled with sunlight and the air no longer carried the cool, musty smell of indoors. The majestic, curving pavilion with its broken skylights and ornate ceiling— that's where they were now.

Thena cried out gratefully—coming here was for the best. She'd never have stayed on Cendrillon's back all the way to the house, and she wouldn't have had the strength or reason to use the radio once she arrived there. Thena shoved herself off Cendrillon's back and collapsed sideways on the cool, smooth floor of the pavilion. She barely knew when she turned to lay on her back, her arms limp by her sides.

The whispers began again. Thena shook her head wearily. No such thing. Jedidiah was right. There were no spirits—why would they have let this awful thing happen if they truly existed outside her imagination? The caring, protective presence around her was part of her imagination, too, but it gave her comfort.

If death is coming, she thought peacefully, this is a good place to meet it. But her face contracted with grief—she didn't want to die, she wanted to hold Jedidiah again, desperately. She wanted to raise the children he would give her and grow old with him.

"Jedidiah, I need you," she begged aloud. Her voice echoed throughout the silent mansion, and she lost consciousness before the echo faded.

It was the merest wisp, more like a memory than a sensation, but he smiled as the clean, flowered scent of Sancia's forest air reached him. Lying on the Bullocks' guest room bed—the same bed he'd shared with Thena two weeks ago—Jed woke quickly when he realized that he wasn't dreaming the island fragrance.

He jacknifed up in bed, wide awake, his eyes searching the room. Late morning sunlight angled through a window to his left, which told him that he'd been napping for at least an hour since the strange incident in the training ring. He inhaled raggedly, his heart thundering in a way that sent needles of fear down his spine. He wasn't dreaming the scent of Sancia's ancient forest. Horror spread through him like a dark cloud. Something was wrong with Thena, and nothing anyone could say would convince him otherwise.

He leapt out of bed, ignoring the soreness in his ribs, grabbing his wallet and boots as he ran toward the door. Downstairs he raced past an archway that led to the home's big den. He caught a glimpse of Barbara doing paperwork at a desk there.

"Goin' to the island!" he yelled, and kept running.

"My lord, Jed, don't. Wait!"

But by the time she ran outside, he was already jerking his black Ferrari into gear. He swung it down the Circle Ten's graveled driveway and had already exceeded the local speed limit by the time the car reached the main road.

Thena was damp and cold with fever already, and she shivered even more as long evening shadows crept off the marshes into the pavilion. In a brief interlude of consciousness, she heard Cendrillon's soft, close nicker. Godiva and Rasputin had pressed their big bodies on either side of Thena's, and she vaguely felt their muzzles resting on her arms.

She was alone, dying alone except for these dear old friends. Jedidiah . . . poor Jedidiah. She loved him so, and it hurt to think of the loneliness he'd suffer without her. She recreated his dear face deep in the last coherent recesses of her mind . . . and he was with her, she knew suddenly. There were no spirits. There was Jedidiah, and all the love between them. Even in the last minutes, she would cherish him. She turned her face toward the magenta shadows and was still.

Jed didn't wait for Farlo's boat to reach Sancia's dock. He jumped across the last four feet.

"I'll wait, just like you said to!" the old fisherman called after him. "But hurry, 'cause the sun's about to set! I don't like this place after dark!"

Jed crossed the beach at a run and headed up the woods path toward Thena's house, his stomach wrenching with fear. It was so damn far. No matter how fast he ran, it was so far. . . .

Godiva and Rasputin's deep barking reached him

only seconds before the two giant dogs leapt across the trail. Jed slid to a halt, his chest heaving as he studied them. They whirled in circles, the barking growing louder and more forceful, then darted down a branch of the trail, stopped, and looked at him expectantly.

"Oh, my God, where is she?" Jed rasped. "Go! Go find Thena!" They took off at a lope, and he sprinted after.

When they broke from the woods and galloped headlong toward SalHaven, glowing in the sunset, Jed halted, uncertain. Here? Not here! If Thena wasn't in this damn place, if he'd wasted precious time coming here to hunt for her when she needed him elsewhere, he'd come back later and tear the old mansion down with his bare hands, stone by stone.

He ran forward through the tall weeds of young pine trees that marked the former lawns. When he reached the curving staircases at SalHaven's entrance, the dogs appeared above him in the dark rectangle of the door. Then he heard the quick rattle of hooves on the marble. Jed gazed up in shock as Cendrillon appeared in the door also, her head tossing wildly.

Thena was here, then. He stumbled up the steps, and the three animals pivoted back toward the mansion's darkening interior. Jed walked swiftly through the shadowy hall.

"Thena! Thena, where are you?" he yelled at the top of his lungs.

His heart, his life, stopped when he looked down the long hallway to the pavilion beyond and saw her lying there, absolutely, deathly still. He was hardly aware of the horrified, begging words that he groaned as he ran to her and collapsed on his knees.

"Dear God, dear God, no," he prayed, when he saw the awful, swollen ankle. One of his big hands grasped her wrist and searched frantically until the callused fingertips found a pulse. Tears of gratitude slid down his face as he gathered her in his arms and lurched to his feet.

"Jedidiah." Her eyes didn't open, but the smile on her face and the sound of her faint voice wrenched a sob from him. "I love you . . . so. Stay with me . . . until I die."

"Sweetheart . . . if you die, I'll go with you." He turned and carried her into the towering hallway, toward Cendrillon, who would carry them both back to Farlo's boat. As he walked, Jed lifted his ravaged face and gazed around the silent old mansion. "I'll take care of her now," he said hoarsely. "Thank you for keepin' her alive for me. I heard you call."

Thena woke to the murmuring sound of Jed's deep voice. She lifted her head and gazed past the tied-back netting at the foot of her bed, then smiled. He sat on the floor by the open window, dressed only in cutoffs, talking amicably to the wrens on the sill. Thena tilted her head in gentle wonder—in all the time he'd spent on Sancia, he'd never conversed with the wrens before. Something cynical and resistant had changed inside him during the past few days, and she didn't understand why.

"Jedidiah, you're unusually appealing and sweet today, you know."

His head jerked around at the sound of her voice. He vaulted to his feet and came to her side of the bed, then bent over her and lovingly cupped her head in his hands. His dark eyes were as warm as the autumn afternoon. "Good nap?" he asked. She nodded. "How does it feel to be back home again?"

Thena shifted her foot a little. It lay out from under the white bedspread, propped on a pillow. She sighed in contentment. "Except for being a little sore, I'm wonderful. Being back on Sancia with you makes me feel perfect." She wrinkled her nose. "The hospital air tasted . . . white."

He chuckled, and her gaze meandered over the bare, taut expanse of his chest and stomach. She put her fingertips on his mouth, then trailed them down his body. His sharp inhalation held delight, but also concern.

"Whoooa," he urged. "You're not well."

"I'm practically well." Her eyes flared with desire. "I believe I'll chase you, if you don't cooperate."

His voice came out husky and very gentle. "I reckon I can't have you doin' that." He slipped his cutoffs to the floor and stretched out, naked, beside her. "Let's go real slow and careful, gal."

"Oh, yes."

He slid the covers off her and eased her short white nightgown—her one concession to being sick—over her head. They nestled deep into each other's arms, touching, kissing, murmuring endearments. The weeks of separation and the restraint demanded by her weak condition combined to charge the mood with tender passion.

After an eternity of slow caresses, Jed settled slowly inside her welcoming body, bringing an ecstatic gleam to her silver eyes. They mesmerized him, and in the delicious, heated moments that followed, he gauged the way they changed, like clouds glowing brighter from the rays of an inner sun, glowing until she and he were both lost in their sheer, luminescent heaven.

Afterwards, he put on his cutoffs again and wrapped her in a blanket, then carried her to the room's big rocker. Jed cradled her in his lap, and they listened to the lazy drone of insects outside and the rustling of the wind in the oaks. Thena nuzzled his neck.

"Jedidiah, you knew I needed you, and you came back. You were right, there aren't any spirits on Sancia. There's the bond between us, and that's all that's important. I think . . . I think I can go with you to Wyoming now. I was wrong to believe in spirits."

"Ssssh, no," he crooned. "Do you want them to hear you and get their feelin's hurt?"

"What? Jedidiah?"

He rested his cheek on her short, dark hair, his eyes thoughtful. It was time to explain what he'd felt the other day. He spoke slowly, his voice reverent, as he explained about the strange happenings that had sent him back to her so frantically. He ended by saying, "They called me back here, Thena. I still believe in the bond between us, but I believe in your spirits too. My . . . grandpa . . . was with them the other day, lookin' out for you . . . and for me."

She leaned back and gave him a silent, richly awed look. Then she whispered, "You belong here. You know that now."

He nodded, looking perplexed. "Is it crazy? I feel welcome now. I feel at home."

She pointed excitedly to her old dresser, an arm's reach away. He helped her up while she searched through the top drawer, and when she'd retrieved a faded, wrinkled photograph, he lifted her into his arms again and sat back in the rocker.

Thena held it out for him to see. "SalHaven, Jedidiah. Before the hurricane." She paused. "I knew you'd want to see a picture, someday."

He studied the magnificent home and lawns that had been SalHaven in its glory days. His breath caught in bittersweet appreciation, and he cleared his throat roughly. "Say, gal, how would you feel about rebuildin' the old place? Can you picture quarter horses grazin' out front, or is that a silly notion?"

For a startled moment Thena stared at him in happy disbelief. Then she threw her arms around his neck and kissed him. "Yes, yes! We'll fill SalHaven with the love it's been waiting for all these years, Jedidiah."

His heart felt as if it would burst from his chest. "I want to see the old place light up with happiness," he told her gruffly. "It'll be our home and our children's home and when we're gone, we'll leave so much love behind that the house won't ever be empty again."

The smile she gave him held an eternity of happiness, and he returned it with all the love in his soul. From deep in the island glades, the wind made a sacred sound, almost like a peaceful sigh.

THE EDITOR'S CORNER

At LOVESWEPT, we believe that the settings for our books can be Anywhere, USA, but we do like to be transported into the lives of the hero and heroine, and into their worlds, and we enjoy it very much when our authors create authentic small town or big city settings for their delicious love stories. This month we'll take you from a farm in Oklahoma, to a resort town on the ocean in New Jersey, to the big cities of Los Angeles, New York, and Chicago, so settle into your favorite traveling armchair and enjoy these new places and new couples in love.

Fran Baker has done a wonderful job recreating the world of the farmer and oilman in **THE WIDOW AND THE WILDCATTER**, #246, a heartwarming and heartwrenching story of love, family, and land. Chance McCoy is a hero you'll love to love. He's strong, gorgeous, adventurous, and available to the woman who needs him to make her and her grandfather's dream come true. What begins as a dream to strike it rich ends as dreams of love are fulfilled for Chance and Joni. Fran Baker certainly does strike it rich in this story!

With our next title, we leave the farmlands of Oklahoma for the New Jersey shore where Cass Lindley, heroine of **SILK ON THE SKIN**, LOVESWEPT #247, owns an exclusive boutique in a resort town, and is the major stockholder of the family's lingerie business. Cass has her hands full of silks, satin, and lace when she discovers that her company is in trouble. M&L Lingerie creates the finest intimate garments for the market but the chairman of the board, Ned Marks, decides they should compete with Fredrick's of Hollywood! Cass is appalled and finally listens to the new president, Dallas Carter, who has a plan to oust Ned. Cass has never mixed business with pleasure but Dallas is too good and too sexy to remain just a professional colleague. They become colleagues in the bedroom as well as the boardroom, pledging a lifelong commitment to each other. Author Linda Cajio has done it again with a sophisticated and sexy love story.

(continued)

Meanwhile, in Los Angeles the subject is real estate, not lingerie. In fact, our heroine is fighting our hero to save her family's ancestral home! **THE OBJECT OF HIS AFFECTION,** LOVESWEPT #248, is another Sara Orwig special. Hilary Wakefield has to resort to dynamite to get Brink Claiborn's attention. It works and the real explosion is the one that happens between them. The gorgeously muscled heartbreaker makes her tremble with smoldering need, and Hilary knows she is flirting with danger by losing her heart to a man she disagrees with on just about everything. But, as usual, Sara Orwig manages to find a common ground for these two lovers who just can't stay away from each other.

January St. John whisks Houston Tyler to an isolated island off the coast of Maine because she's desperate to see the man who stole her heart after only a brief but intense encounter. So begins **JANUARY IN JULY,** LOVESWEPT #249, by Joan Elliott Pickart, and from beginning to end one of your favorite LOVESWEPT authors brings you a love affair to rival any other. January is very wealthy and Houston is a working man—a man who uses his hands and his body in his work and it shows! They come from different worlds but once their hearts touch one another, social differences dissolve. In their island hideaway, they have the opportunity to savor kisses and explore the fireworks that their love creates. They're sensational together, and nothing else matters. Thank you Joan!

LET'S DO IT AGAIN, LOVESWEPT #250, is a first book for us by a new LOVESWEPT author, Janet Bieber. You are all probably familiar with the successful writing team Janet Joyce which has published twenty romances. Well, Janet Bieber was half of that team and now she's gone solo with **LET'S DO IT AGAIN.** So, do give a warm welcome to Janet! I'm sure you're going to enjoy her wonderful story of two lovers who can't let their divorce stand in the way of their love. **LET'S DO IT AGAIN** is about starting over. It's about two adults who have the rare opportunity to learn from their mistakes and build a stronger relationship the second time around. Dave St. Claire returns from traveling the globe determined to

(continued)

convince his ex-wife, Maggie, that they should get rid of that "ex." Dave has realized that a happy family life is really what's important, but meanwhile Maggie has built a life of her own without her wandering husband. But electricity is still there sizzling beneath the surface, and his sweet addictive kisses have grown more potent with time. They get to know each other again, emotionally and physically, and Maggie finally believes his promises. After all, a piece of paper didn't make them stop loving one another!

We end the month appropriately with **THE LUCK OF THE IRISH** by Patt Bucheister, LOVESWEPT #251, a story about trusting and allowing love to grow when you're lucky enough to find it. When Kelly McGinnis first spotted the mysterious woman stepping out of a limousine, he thought of soft music, moonlit nights, and satin sheets! Clare Denham tantalized him with her charm and humor. Clare felt dangerously attracted to the Irishman who had kissed the Blarney Stone and now had powers she couldn't fight. Why fight it when falling in love is the most glorious experience of a lifetime? Patt Bucheister convinced her characters to take the plunge, and I, for one, am glad she did!

We've discovered that in our recent Editor's Corners we accidentally called Kay Hooper's incredible hero, Joshua Long by the wrong last name. I just want to clarify that the dashing and virile Joshua Long is the hero of the "Hagen Strikes Again" series from Kay Hooper.

Enjoy!
Sincerely,

Kate Hartson

Kate Hartson
    Editor
LOVESWEPT
Bantam Books.
666 Fifth Avenue
New York, NY 10103